I0520409

Demon Bringer
Darkshield Volume I
By Kathe Todd

Chapter 1

There was a crashing, rending sound, and Adara's eyes popped open. She had dropped off to sleep only an hour before on her little cot in the tiny second bedroom of her family's cottage a short distance from the banks of the Willough river. What had happened?

After tucking her in Mama had left the door ajar, so that she and Papa could hear if their little daughter cried out in the night. Eyes wide in fright, Adara crept toward that door and peered out through the crack. She could see down the hall to the front door, which appeared to have been smashed open, and she could see figures – monstrous figures – coming in through it. There were so many of them that several waited for their companions to clear the entryway before they could come through, and they were easily visible by the light of the oil lamp that hung on the wall of the hallway.

Her heart was beating so fast it was like a caged bird fluttering to escape, as Adara beheld the creatures who had come into their little home, and heard what had to be her mother and father screaming in terror – and pain. "No, stop! Don't hurt her, you monster!" Papa's voice rang out. Then there was a woman's scream, and an inarticulate cry from Papa accompanied by the sound of something hard striking flesh.

What *were* they? They were big – well, maybe not as big as Papa. When you're six years old everyone but your fellow children looks big. They were shaped roughly like men, standing on two legs and holding swords and axes in their two hands. But their arms were too long, their legs too short for their massively muscled bodies – and their faces, what Adara could see of them beneath the helmets they wore, looked like the snouts of wild animals. They had piggy little yellow eyes, no whites showing, and tusks protruded from their lower jaws. They were grunting and squealing to each other in some guttural language, or maybe it was just animal noises.

Adara realized that urine was running down her legs. In her terror, she had wet herself. She very quietly shut her bedroom door and threw the latch. She had to get away! Stepping out of the drawers she'd been wearing beneath her nightdress, she went to the window. The casement opened outward, and in another few seconds she had

3

climbed through it and was running, barefoot, away to the west behind the cottage.

It was very dark out here, three miles downstream from the village, and Adara didn't think she would be able to find her way there. But she had lived here all her life, and she could certainly find her way in the darkness north to the river road and across it to the small jetty where the Willoughby family kept their little fishing skiff. The current here was slow, and Papa was able to row up and down the river at need – catching fish to sell in town and more to put on their table. He'd taken Adara with him on several occasions, and she'd learned to swim almost before she could walk.

After getting to the other side of the road she risked a look back at the house. The door was still open, and there were shadows being cast out the front window by the lamp in the room that did duty for cooking, dining, and sitting. That was where Mama and Papa usually spent the evenings, reading books by lamplight, performing small chores like mending, or just talking quietly.

The screams had subsided, though the pig-men were still brandishing their weapons. With a gasp, tears streaming unnoticed down her cheeks, Adara dashed to the jetty and cast off the single line that kept the boat bobbing at its moorings – then jumped inside. Seizing one of the oars, she pushed off from the dock and the little boat glided out into the current. She lacked the size and strength to use the oarlocks, but she could paddle with the current. In another minute she and the skiff were lost in the darkness, moving downstream.

Chapter 2

The weather had cleared, and Nanny Selden was out with her collecting bag. With summer coming on, more plants were beginning to bloom and she had a mental list of a dozen or more she intended to harvest this day. Despite the sobriquet, she was not a grandmother – though at fifty-seven she was certainly old enough for the job. Yet she and her Bill had never had any children, and he'd been dead these past thirty years in any case.

But the residents of the village of Pine Hill insisted on calling her that. She was their herb wife, the woman who provided them with what medical care they received. The potions she concocted could ease a difficult pregnancy or prevent one altogether, keep a wound from festering, give one a boost in health and energy after a winter spent shut inside.

More than one of her customers had urged her to move closer to town, as the two-mile trip to her clearing in the pine woods east of the bustling village could be a hardship if help was needed in the wintertime. But she valued her privacy, and loved her little cottage with its view of a meadow that now, in late spring, was a riot of colorful wildflowers – most of them valuable ingredients for her potions. If they wanted what she had to offer, let them come to her.

After passing through some narrow rapids upstream the Willough, in this stretch of its journey toward its confluence with the far-larger Grandeon – another hundred miles to the west – ran relatively slow and wide. In the occasional meanders cattails and other aquatic plants grew, and now that Nanny had picked as many flowers as she needed she was heading for the riverbank. She needed some of the new green cattails, and hoped to find some older ones as well. Not every plant she collected was destined to become medicine – some of them were food, or had other uses.

As Nanny came within sight of the water she stopped dead and squinted. Truthfully, her old eyes were not what they once had been. Was that a *boat* nudged into shore, caught among the reeds? Yes, it was! A sturdily built, flat-bottomed skiff around twelve feet long, squared off so that bow and stern were the same, and with a pair of iron oarlocks that must have cost a pretty penny mounted in the rails that ran along the sides. But there were no oars in sight.

Nanny considered her footwear. She'd likely have been getting muddy in any case, picking cattails. She pulled off her boots and lifted her full skirt up, tucking it into the waistband so that it came up above her knees. If this boat hadn't been lost by someone in Pine Grove, she'd be able to sell it for a good price.

Her collecting bag slung over her shoulder to leave her hands free, Nanny waded carefully out into the shallow water. She placed each bare foot gingerly, well aware that there were things in the mud here that could give you a nasty cut if you didn't mind where you stepped. Then she reached the skiff and gasped as she saw what lay in the bottom of it. A little girl, and it looked as if she might dead!

Chapter 3

A rope was attached to the end of the craft furthest from the shore, dangling in the water, and Nanny waded out until she was in danger of getting her skirt wet and seized it in her strong right hand. Then she heaved on it, pulling the lightweight, sled-like craft around and hauling it up out of the water. The reeds bent and it glided over them until it had reached the firmer ground of shore. And as it jolted to a halt, the girl stirred. Alive!

In another moment Nanny had put her boots back on and was stooping to lift the child from where she lay in the bottom of the boat. There were no oars, no food or water, nothing but the child herself and a small anchor attached to a thin chain. And the girl, who surely could not be more than six, looked wan and wasted. She was clad in only a thin, stained nightdress.

Nanny judged the boat would not be going anywhere, not that she cared about that now. She needed to get this child back to her cottage before the little one expired from starvation and exposure! She always been a tall, strong woman ("Built like a brick shithouse," her Bill had said fondly) and she had no trouble making all speed with this slight burden in her arms. Within ten minutes she was unlocking her front door, and carrying the little waif inside.

The old woman laid the unconscious child down on the small bed she kept in the cottage's main room. From time to time, she might need to nurse a patient here for a few days and nights. Quickly she stoked up the fire and got a kettle on, then gathered the ingredients for a special tea. The girl would need broth, and as much nourishment as she could take on; but first, she must be rehydrated. From the sunken appearance of her skin, Nanny guessed she'd had nothing to drink for a day or two.

The child's nightdress unbuttoned down the front, and her caretaker opened it up to check for any signs of injury. There were none – no wounds, no bruises. But she got a sharp frisson as she realized that the nightdress was not the only thing the girl was wearing. Around her neck she had a circlet, a little bigger than a choker, which seemed to be made of some mysterious liquid metal. It was flexible, matte black in color, and showed no sign of chain links.

In the center of the band's widest part was a cabochon stone half an inch in diameter. It appeared to be as black at the metal of the band, in the relatively dim light of the cottage's front room – though there were hints and glints of other hues in its clear depths. There was magic here, Nanny knew, and wondered at it. She was not precisely a sorceress, as her world knew such things; but she had her insights and her powers. Most of these were completely unknown to the people of Pine Hill, who thought that all she achieved was worked by the herbs in her potions.

The girl's limbs were stick-thin, her head covered in a tousled mop of jet-black hair though her skin was pale. But from the look of her, this thinness might well have been the result of starvation during her journey by boat. She appeared to have been well cared for up until recently, so it was likely she had not run away from home. What had happened, to send her on a near-fatal journey down the Willough?

In a few minutes the tea had brewed, and Nanny had cooled it to a little above room temperature with a whispered request to Ariel, spirit of the wind. In the meantime she had re-buttoned the girl's nightdress so that she was decently covered again. There had been no sign of a means to remove the mysterious necklace, and Nanny suspected that it had been placed there for the child's protection. Best to leave it alone.

Holding the child up into a sitting position with her left arm, the old woman began feeding sips of the tea to her patient. After a couple of swallows, the girl showed signs of returning energy and actively began drinking the tea; though her eyes remained closed.

Nanny propped her up on some cushions and refilled the mug from the pot, the contents of which had now cooled. As she turned back to the bed, she found a pair of enormous blue eyes staring at her in wonder. "Oh good, you're awake!" she said matter-of-factly. "Here, drink some more of this tea. Then I'll see about getting you something to eat. I suppose you're pretty hungry."

The eyes blinked, then the girl lifted her hands to the mug and downed its contents thirstily. Nanny had sweetened it with honey, adding a little nutrition to the energizing and hydrating effects of the tea, and when the girl had emptied the mug she said. "Thank you. Can I have some more?"

Nanny poured another mug, emptying the pot. "Just one more," she said reprovingly, "and don't gulp it. Just drink it slowly, or you may make yourself sick."

"All right," the little one said, and took only a single sip before looking around her and asking "Who are you, and where am I?"

"I'm Mrs. Selden, but everyone calls me Nanny," the old woman replied. "This is my cottage, near Pine Hill on the banks of the Willough." That last name triggered a memory. The Willough! That was where they lived, they were the Willoughby family. They... there was a sudden chaotic mental image of armed and armored figures swarming in through a broken door to the accompaniment of screams, and her mind retreated.

"And what's your name, dear?" Nanny asked sweetly. I know that one, the girl thought, and said "Adara. Adara Willoughby." Willoughby, the old woman thought. But the Willough was hundreds of miles long. And in this modern age, when family names were becoming more common in the kingdom of Tanar, just because your family had taken a place name didn't necessarily mean they still lived there.

Was there a town by that name? Nanny had lived her whole life in the Pine Hill area and had never been further away from it than fifty miles up or down stream. She knew that the Willough flowed into the Grandeon, and that *that* mighty river bisected the kingdom of Tanar between north and south, running from its eastern border in the Crestan Mountains to the Westwater a thousand miles away. And that at the mouth of the Grandeon stood Carlienne, Tanar's capital and the site of King Arden's court. But other than that, her notions of geography were sketchy. It was not a subject that had much application in people's daily lives.

Adara had continued sipping at the now-cooled tea, and she was feeling ever so much better. "Did you say there was something to eat?" she asked hopefully, and Nanny gave her a broad grin. She had baked a loaf of apple bread just yesterday, and there was still half of it left. She cut off a few slices and slathered them with some peach preserves she'd made last summer, then brought a tray. Adara sat up unaided and attacked the food with a will, and Nanny brought her a mug of spring water to wash it down with – smiling to herself. Clearly, her little patient was going to live.

Nanny waited until Adara had eaten as much as she could, and was surprised at how much that was. Now, she said gently, "Adara, I found you in a small skiff washed up in the shallows along the banks of the Willough. How did you come to be there, and where did you come from? Where are your family?" The little one looked at her with those big blue eyes, a haunted expression on her face. "I can't remember," she said.

Chapter 4

"You have everything?" Nanny asked, looking up at the tall young woman who now, at what she thought was probably seventeen, overtopped her by more than an inch. Adara grinned at her fondly. Her foster mother was getting old, certainly – nearly seventy, she claimed – but she was still as sharp as a tack. It was a good thing her young apprentice had no intention of trying to put anything over on her.

She hefted the straps of the pack on her back. "The arthritis salve goes to Albert Miller, the tonic to Mrs. Fletcher, the rest to Mrs. Green for the store as usual." Years ago now, when Adara had gotten old enough to start making the trip into Pine Hill by herself, they'd struck a deal with the widow who ran the village's general store to stock Nanny's most popular potions there. It saved a lot of trips back and forth, and everyone was happy with the arrangement.

Nanny nodded approvingly, and Adara went on. "I'm to pick up a half side of bacon from the smokehouse, some corn from Mr. Miller for the hens, and six yards of the blue cotton fabric from Mrs. Green. Did I miss anything?" The older woman gave her a squeeze and a peck on the cheek.

"You've got it down perfectly, dear," she assured the girl who had changed her life. "And watch out for that young scamp Jason Miller. That boy's up to no good!"

Adara kissed her back and went smilingly on her way. It was a lovely day for a walk into town, early spring sunshine doing battle with some rain clouds that looked like they might probably give up the fight. And if not, she had her hooded cloak to keep off any unexpected showers. As she walked along the well-beaten path through the pine woods toward town, her thoughts turned toward Jason Miller.

Nanny was right, she knew. He was a cutie, and she felt her heart beat faster whenever she watched him hauling sacks of grain with his shirt off; but his protestations of love had never gotten to the point of asking her to be his wife. She might have all the herb lore she needed to avoid an unwanted pregnancy, but for some reason Adara was holding onto her maidenhood at an age when most village girls had long since become matrons. Jason wasn't the only Pine Hill boy who'd tried to get into her pants, either – though by the standards of her time Adara's tall, lanky build was not considered particularly desirable. Boys wanted girls who were soft, round, and cuddly.

Ah well, Adara thought with a sigh. There was plenty of time left in her life to find romance. And in the meantime she had a valuable trade, one with which she could support herself almost anywhere. Perhaps it might be enjoyable to go out and see something of the world, before settling down. In the past nearly eleven years, since Nanny had found the starving and mysterious waif washed up on the shores of the river near her cottage, she had taught the girl nearly everything she knew – including the ways in which the elemental spirits of earth, air, fire, and water could be cajoled into lending one a hand.

As she left the woods behind and followed the trail to the outskirts of the village, Adara idly fingered the necklace she wore. Nanny had been very curious about it, but she'd been unable to tell her much. She had a dim memory of a woman who must have been her mother putting it around her neck, and telling her that it would protect her and she must never take it off.

But the trauma of whatever event it was that had led to Adara's journey downriver had driven all of her earliest memories away. Sometimes she had unsettling dreams, and when she'd been little they were horrendous, blood-soaked nightmares that had brought her awake screaming. Nanny had been there by her side, hugging her tight and driving away all her fears. And these days such fleeting memories rarely troubled her anymore.

Adara arrived in Pine Hill and made her away along the central street, cobblestone paved, that ran from the docks at the riverside up over a rise to the sawmill. She was greeted cheerfully by everyone she met, for Nanny Selden's young ward and apprentice was a pretty girl as well as being kindly and good at the job she'd been trained to.

After running her errands in town Adara turned down a side street, which wound out nearly a mile from the river to where the Miller place sat on a good-sized creek. Here the local farmers brought their grain to be ground into flour, the massive stones turned by water power from the stream.

"Good day, Mr. Miller," Adara called out as she spotted the elder miller at work. Though he was only in his forties, Albert Miller had fallen prey to swollen and painful joints, and the salve Nanny Selden (or sometimes, Adara herself) crafted for him greatly helped to ease the pain. The ingredients and method of preparation were Nanny's own invention, a closely guarded secret known only to the two of them.

After the sacks of grain had been put into the hopper, the miller came down to greet her with a smile on his face. "Good day Adara," he said fondly. "You're looking well." His younger son Jason, aged nineteen, was over there like a shot as soon as he heard her name.

Midday was almost upon them. "Can I take a lunch break, Papa?" the young man asked, and his father (having received the salve and handed over the sack of cracked corn along with some coins in payment) nodded with a rueful smile. He wasn't sure what his son's intentions were regarding the girl, but he hoped trouble was not going to come of it. Ah, why worry? Adara was a bright lass, and she seemed to be capable of looking out for herself.

"Let me carry that grain for you, Adara," Jason told her as he fell into step behind. "Can I buy you some lunch at the Loggers' Rest before you go home?" he asked hopefully. She eyed him sideways with a little smile.

"I don't know," she said. "*Can* you?" He grinned at her and pulled out a little purse, jingling it to show it had more than a coin or two inside.

"Certainly can!" he declared, and they set off together on the road to town.

The loggers for whom the place had been named could be a rowdy bunch of an evening, especially if they'd just been paid; but the village's only tavern was a quiet and respectable enough place at lunchtime. They took a small table near the fireplace, which was cold at this hour, and Martha brought them bowls of a venison stew rich with carrots and potatoes, and a bit of bacon to give it some fat. The pine woods abounded with game, but at this season it was pretty lean and stringy. They washed it down with flagons of the house's excellent small beer.

"So Adara," Jason said as he put down his flagon and dipped a hunk of fresh black bread into his stew, "I was hoping you might be willing to accompany me to the Spring Dance at Harlings' barn." This annual event was the start of what passed for a social season in Pine Hill, the first public get-together since Longnight.

Next would come Quickening, with outdoor festivities, then Longday. Games and celebrations would go on all afternoon, with a huge fire over which a whole bullock would be roasted, and far into the night for the adults at least. Any sparking couples who had not managed to get together by Harvest had best forget about it.

But the Spring Dance wasn't until the end of this month, and Adara was not sure. It might be more fun just to go together with Nanny, and be free to dance with *all* the boys. She liked Jason, and she was attracted to him. But she didn't feel there was any big connection between them. Most girls in Pine Hill were happy to hook up with whatever reasonably good looking, provident young fellow showed an interest in them, get married and start popping out fat babies as they settled into the same sort of lives that their mothers and grandmothers had lived before them. But shouldn't there be something more to life?

Adara smiled slightly and concentrated on her stew for a while. Mm, it was good! They ate a lot of chicken, and sometimes rabbits or squirrels Adara got with her bow, at Nanny's place. But the richness of red meat was a rare treat. She looked forward to having some of that bacon with the eggs that were a daily staple of their diets.

Jason was watching her, a curious expression of half-hidden longing on his face, and it occurred to Adara he was waiting for an answer. "Thanks for the invitation, Jason," she said sweetly. "But I'm not sure. I'll need to talk it over with Nanny before I can tell you yes or no." The old lady made a handy excuse, and his face fell. It seemed to Jason that at Adara's age she ought to be making her own decisions, not tied to Nanny's apron strings. But Nanny had been a figure of note and power in the area for as long as he could remember. He wasn't about to argue.

Instead, he squeezed her hand and looked into those beautiful blue eyes. His gaze strayed down from there to her chest, where the tops of her generous (for a woman so slender) breasts could just be seen above her blouse. Adara followed that gaze, then pulled her hand free from his and slapped it lightly. "Mind your manners, Jason!" she said sternly, and he flushed.

"Well, back to the grind," Jason quipped as he took leave of Adara outside the tavern. She grinned at him.

"I'll see you next time I'm in town for supplies," she promised, giving him a kiss on the cheek. It was as intimate as they'd yet gotten, though a time or two she'd fantasized about locking her mouth on his to see what it felt like. She had never been *really* kissed. She hefted the pack with its heavy contents up onto her back, and set off along the path for home.

Chapter 5

Adara knew there was trouble as soon as she saw the smoke rising above the trees, just as she was just entering the outskirts of the pine woods. That was *way* too much smoke for the fireplace at Nanny's cottage to be putting out, on this warm afternoon in early spring!

The pack was heavy, but Adara was strong and she sprang into a ground-eating lope as she toiled the nearly two miles through the woods to the clearing. What would she find? By the time she got there, though, the smoke had mostly faded away.

Adara burst into the clearing and ran to the cottage. The door was open, and as she came inside and shed her pack she realized it had been smashed in. The interior was a shambles – foodstuffs, crockery, potion ingredients scattered all over the place as if a whirlwind had swept through. "Nanny!" she called out anxiously. "Nanny, where are you?" A mounting terror was threatening to overwhelm her, a terror she had felt before.

"Adara!" came a faint cry from the rear of the cottage, and the young woman found the old woman down on the floor of the hallway between her bedroom and the storeroom that had become Adara's, trying to rise.

"Nanny, what happened?!" Adara cried out, giving her a hand. The old woman's nearly-white hair was disheveled, and there was a bleeding lump on the side of her head. More blood was running from what looked like a knife cut in her right forearm.

Adara hugged the old woman to her breast, then helped her down the hall to sit on the same small bed where she herself had lain when Nanny had first found her – nearly dead from hunger, thirst, and exposure. In moments she had water on, and was assembling the ingredients needed to treat Nanny's injuries.

Five minutes later the cut and head injury had been cleaned and bandaged, the latter with a poultice to reduce swelling and the former with several stitches in it. That cut had been deep! Nanny was finishing a cup of tea, and seemed recovered enough at last to tell Adara what had befallen her.

"They came right around midday, while I was tending the henhouse," Nanny said. "I've never seen anything like them. Maybe five and a half feet tall, like a cross between a man, an ape, and a pig! They were all dressed in armor and livery the way the duke's soldiers are, but it wasn't anything like his. They had a three-headed beast on their surcoats, with a glaring eye above it."

Adara went white. Suddenly the gates of her memory were opened up, and she was six years old again. The noise, the screaming and shouting, the animal cries, Mama and Papa... She swayed on her feet. Nanny hadn't noticed. "They all had swords and axes," she went on. "And one of 'em got me on the arm. But I got them, too!" she crowed fiercely. "Little bastards didn't know what hit 'em!"

Adara shook herself out of her panic. She was *not* six years old anymore, and there were apparently no foes here. "Salomand?" she guessed, and Nanny nodded. The spirit of fire was volatile – easily brought to your aid, but once he had been invoked it was sometimes hard to stop him before things got out of hand. Usually, they only asked his help for lighting fires in the fireplace – and occasionally, oil lamps.

"Three of them fell and the fourth one ran off screaming," Nanny went on, showing a surprising amount of nasty satisfaction for a sweet old lady of advanced years. "But the damned henhouse caught on fire. I ran to the spring to get some water to throw on it, too far for Onden to help. And then, just as I got the flames out and was inspecting the bodies, some more of them showed up. I ran into the house and barred the door," – she glanced ruefully at it, realizing it would need to be rebuilt before it could be locked again – "but they came right through it. I guess I'm lucky to be alive."

"Rest, Nanny!" Adara admonished. She had to go outside and see for herself. There might be no immediate threat, but her mind was roiling with memories of deadly peril. It was all, finally, coming back. She stepped around the side of the cottage to the henhouse in the back. The hens were off about their daily business, foraging for bugs and plant foods in the meadow. They would all return at dusk and be locked up tight by nightfall, safe from marauding foxes and stoats.

The fire hadn't been too bad. A portion of the wall from around four feet above the ground to the roof on the right side, opposite the ramp up which the chickens went to get inside, was blackened. But it didn't seem to have collapsed. Probably the hens would still be able to shelter here for the night.

But what riveted Adara's attention was the bodies. Seemingly, the pig-man soldiers had *not* retrieved their dead. In today's unseasonably warm conditions the corpses were already beginning to smell. Or maybe they'd smelled like that to begin with!

Two of the bodies had caught fire and were charred to the point where it was hard to make out any details. They gave off a gut-churning odor that was a combination of barbecued pork and rotting flesh. But the third one was face-down, the fire having only burned its backside. It must have died from the shock of intense pain.

Biting her lip, her face a mask of revulsion, Adara put out a booted foot and pushed until the corpse lifted and rolled over onto its back. Mother Maridem save us! Every tiny detail of that night nearly eleven years before came hurtling back with the force of an avalanche, sweeping away the blockage and restoring to her at last those memories – and all that had come before them.

Overcome, Adara sank to her knees. Tears pouring down her cheeks, she pulled her dagger from its sheath at her belt and began cutting away the pig-man's surcoat. It was exactly as she remembered it. These creatures, hirelings of whoever owned that device, were the same ones who had invaded her home and murdered her parents more than half her life ago!

Chapter 6

Nanny was already well on the mend, the herbs' potency and her own natural resilience fighting off any lingering effects of the wounds dealt by the armed invaders. She had been listening with great interest to all Adara was now able to tell her about her earlier life. "What about the necklace?" she asked. The strange – and apparently quite benign – artifact had puzzled her since she had first seen it. It appeared to have grown over the years with its wearer, for it still fit the grown Adara's neck as it had done when she was a child.

"Mama told me it was a family heirloom," the girl replied. The sight of the dead invader had eradicated the blockage, giving her access to even her earliest memories. "She said it would protect me from harm, and that I must never take it off until it was time to give it to someone I loved enough that I was willing to die for them. I didn't understand what she meant – I was only around five at the time."

Somehow the recovered memories had been handed to her as if they were transcripts, and Adara was able to pick things from them that had gotten completely past her child's mind at the time the memories had been formed. It was almost as if they had happened to someone else.

"Take it off?" Nanny prompted. Adara sat lost in thought for a moment, then reached up behind her neck. There, and there! She brought her hands back around in front of her, each holding an end of the now-separated necklace. The old woman goggled.

"I think it can only be removed, and only replaced, by the conscious will of the person wearing it," the girl said. She fastened it around her neck again. There was no sound, but now the necklace was once again a continuous band of dark, faintly shimmering metal.

Nanny shook her head. This was lore beyond anything *she* had ever learned. "Are you certain your parents are dead?" she asked, a hint of guilt in the question. If she had been more diligent, might she not have quested upriver for the parents of this foundling child – and the owners of the long-since-sold skiff?

"They were screaming, and then there were some very unpleasant noises and the screaming stopped," Adara replied. Again, she had the feeling that she was looking at her own memories from a remove. They had somehow lost the power to destroy her emotionally. "If Mama and Papa had survived, wouldn't they have searched for me?" she asked.

"With the skiff gone, it would have been logical to assume that I had taken it and gone downriver," Adara went on without waiting for an answer. "I lost the first oar an hour downstream, then the second one when I came to the first rapids. I suppose it was Maridem's blessing that I survived the rapids and made it here. But it seems likely that Mama and Papa were killed, and that when our neighbors discovered their bodies they assumed I had been taken by whoever had broken into the house and killed them."

Nanny sighed. She had expected that Adara, who had spent most of her life in the environs of Pine Grove, would marry and settle down to live the rest her life here as well – eventually taking over as the community's herb wife and caring for her mentor in whatever years Nanny had left. Now, she was coming to realize that the girl had another calling.

"Mayor Demby will likely have maps, that can tell you how far it is to Willoughby," Nanny said. Adara gave a dismissive wave.

"Willoughby is in my past," she said. An iron resolve seemed to have begun forming within the young woman within minutes after she had reclaimed her memories. "I need to take these arms to someone who can tell me whose they are, track down the duke or whoever he is that sent the pig-men to my home – now and eleven years ago." She flourished the rectangle of cloth cut from the dead soldier's surcoat.

Nanny looked down at her lap, a profound sadness taking her. She was still a woman of iron will, but she was nearly seventy years old. And wounded, and tired. Facing the loss of the blithe girl who had stepped into her life and transformed it was something she wasn't sure she was up for, just now.

In an instant Adara had closed the distance between them, and was enfolding the older woman in her strong arms. "Oh, Nanny!" she cried, "You have been more my mother than my real mother ever got a chance to be! I won't leave you forever. But I have to find out who sent these monstrosities. Can't you see? No one has ever heard of them, ever seen them. Yet they turn up at my house when I'm a child, and again at the place where I'm living all these years later! They must be after *me*, yet somehow they are not able to pinpoint my location. I need to know why, know who sent them – and I need to put a stop to them once and for all. Otherwise I, and everyone I love, will be in danger forever!"

"You're right, dear," Nanny said, hugging her back. The child had cut through to the heart of it, and she had the feeling that the necklace was somehow involved. "If you don't mean to return to Willoughby, I think you should go to Carlienne. There, if anywhere in Tanar, you will find someone who will tell you what you need to know."

Chapter 7

Tears running down her cheeks, Adara hugged Nanny as if she never meant to let go. "Are you sure you'll be all right?" she asked anxiously. In her memories the old woman had been a towering figure, the source of all strength and power. But now, looking down at her, she realized that somehow her beloved foster mother had become... old.

Nanny drew herself up to her full height, still tall for a woman though she'd shrunk an inch or two in the last decade. She put an arm around the twelve-year-old girl who stood beside her. "I'll be perfectly fine," she assured Adara. "Ellie will be coming every day to see to my needs, and learning to make the potions so I don't have to do them all myself. You go to Carlienne and find out what you need to know, and be safe. Don't take that necklace off!"

Adara put a hand to the necklace, now hidden beneath the leather jerkin she wore over her blouse. She was clad in matching pants with sturdy boots – traveling clothes – and armed with a dagger as well as her bow and a quiver full of the finest arrows Arnulf Smith could provide. Most of his work with his customers in Pine Hill and its environs involved lumbering tools and agricultural implements, but he had done some work as an armorer in his youth. A generation ago, young men from all over the duchy had been mustered to join then-King Johan XI in ousting the invading elves of Elyrion from Tanar's western shore.

They were standing in the Pine Hill town square, surrounded by well-wishers, and tears welled up in Adara's eyes again as she considered the love, kindness, and generosity she had been shown by everyone. They had even donated a horse to her – a fifteen-year-old gelding who had retired from pulling a plough, to be sure, but still a horse! She had a purse of money from Nanny, with which it was planned she would take passage on a river boat once she reached the Grandeon.

Adara was loaded down as well with travel rations, water skins, potions, and a map provided by Mayor Demby. It showed the entire kingdom of Tanar, with the major towns and cities and the more important waterways including both the Grandeon and the Willough. Neither Willoughby nor Pine Hill appeared on it, however.

After Adara had hugged several more people and thanked them, Jason Smith enfolded her in a firm embrace and then (to her shock and embarrassment) planted a kiss on her lips right there in front of everyone. She looked at him wide-eyed. There had been a lot of heat in that kiss, and it was making her wish she had been a little less stand-offish. Mmm…

He lifted her up so she could get her foot in the stirrup and climb up onto Bulo's broad back, nearly six feet off the ground. Adara had scarcely ever ridden until recently, but she'd received enough lessons in the past week that she felt she could now handle the placid old fellow without falling off. She shook up the reins, put her heels into his flanks as she'd been taught, and he set off at a fast walk – his "feathered," dinner-plate-size hooves clopping loudly on the cobblestones as he made his way down the road toward the riverside.

Adara turned in the saddle and waved at the crowd as they watched her go. "Goodbye, everyone!" she called. "I'll write when I get a chance!" They all waved in response, then she turned her head forward. Soon she steered the enormous piebald gelding to the left, heading approximately west along the banks of the Willough. The path hardly deserved the name of road, but it was not a game trail either.

Excitement and trepidation were rising in Adara's breast as she considered the enormity of what she was doing. She, an untried young maiden, was setting off by herself on a journey of more than five hundred miles, going to one of the largest cities on the continent to seek out the identity of the enemy who had murdered her family and repeatedly tried to (so she assumed) kill her as well. And that was only the first part of her quest. After she found out who it was, she would then have to do something about him!

Chapter 8

Ferdyn Longblade sat with his back against the bole of an enormous oak tree, and took one final pull from his water skin. He hoped he'd find a spring soon to replenish his water supply, as he doubted it would be a good idea to drink from the waters of the river a hundred paces off to his left. Too many horses, cattle, and assorted other livestock shitting in it, he was sure.

Sighing at the thought of horses, he got his feet under him – brushing the crumbs of his recent luncheon from his greaves – and shouldered his pack once again. If only those damned bandits had not shot his horse out from under him as he was approaching their lair! By the time he had dealt with the half dozen bandits, who were attacking in force, the horse had lost too much blood and he'd had to put her out of her misery.

Now he was afoot on this gods-forsaken excuse for a road, and it was another hundred miles to the Grandeon and his first opportunity catch a boat ride back to Carlienne. At least he'd come out of that encounter with more than enough gold to pay for his passage, and to buy another horse – but it scarcely seemed worthwhile buying one for this awkward week-long journey. There were times, he thought, when the life of a bold adventurer seemed less like a thrilling saga and more like a giant pain in the ass.

He grinned to himself ruefully as he slid Virago into her back sheath beneath the pack. The slender, deadly longsword had been his prize from his first successful venture – raiding the supposedly haunted tomb of a long-dead warlord, when he was all of nineteen and convinced of his own immortality. That success had given him both his sobriquet and a thirst for plunder that had stayed sharp for the past eight years as his skills grew ever greater.

Ferdyn shook his head, seeking to chase his mood away. He was just tired of walking, disgruntled about the loss of his mount. Collecting the bounty offered by the Duke of Rivermarch for cleaning out those bandits would have to wait 'til another time, for he didn't plan to backtrack a hundred miles up the Grandeon to claim it.

As he was about to set off walking again, Ferdyn suddenly heard the sound of heavy hooves coming down the track. He quickly stepped off the road and slipped behind the tree he'd been leaning against earlier, peering out around it. He pulled the brown rough-spun cowl up over his leather helmet, shadowing his face and helping him to blend in with the forest shadows.

Ferdyn's warm brown eyes widened as he beheld the rider approaching. It was no destrier, as he'd thought possible, but an enormous and moth-eaten piebald plough horse. It was moving right along at a fast walk, and showed no signs of expiring from old age, at least. And mounted on its back was a tall, slim girl dressed in traveling leathers, her long silken black hair flowing behind her. She was wearing a green felt forester's cap with a jay feather tucked into it, and had a decent-looking longbow slung across her back. As she drew closer, he realized that she was beautiful.

Bulo shied as a tall man suddenly appeared from behind a tree a few paces from the path. He was wearing leather armor studded with steel plates, and looked to be maybe in his middle twenties. A highwayman? Alarmed, Adara quickly whipped an arrow out of her quiver and drew her bow. Keeping it strung wasn't a great idea, but she had wanted to be ready to address any threats – as well as any little four-footed opportunities that might present themselves.

The stranger hastily pulled off his hood to reveal he had a shoulder-length mop of sandy blond hair beneath a leather helmet of the type that Tanar forces had worn twenty years ago during the so-called Elvany War. He grinned at her, a winningly boyish expression, and held up both hands. He had a long dagger at his belt and an impressively large sword sticking up over his right shoulder where it hung at his back, so the "I'm not armed" gesture wasn't all that believable. But she lowered the bow.

"What do you want?" Adara asked tensely. "Don't make any false moves or I'll shoot," she added in a tone she hoped was menacing. Actually she could have requested Salomand to set this fellow on fire and he probably would have done it – he was always eager to be fed – but she couldn't just go around incinerating people. Besides, it might start a forest fire.

"Fear not, fair lady!" the man replied. "I intend you no harm. I am Ferdyn, known as Longblade, and I am an honest adventurer – slaying bandits, retrieving stolen property, exploring ancient ruins, and so forth. Regrettably my horse was killed during my last encounter with bandits, and I am now afoot. Might I ask whither you are bound?"

He spoke courteously enough, and certainly didn't seem to fit Adara's (admittedly, naïve) notion of what a bandit highwayman would be like. He was too young to have fought in the Elvany War, but she'd be willing to bet that his armor dated from that era – a few years before she'd been born. It was quite well worn, but had clearly received a lot of care and attention. And he was *cute*! Well, perhaps cute wasn't the right word. Jason Smith was cute. This Ferdyn was a man grown, tall and powerful, and he had something that reached out to her and hit her in the crotch like nothing she had ever experienced. Whoa!

The sun was past its height and Adara had been thinking about stopping to eat some lunch. She was getting stiff from riding, and she needed to pee. But she'd been a little anxious that, once she climbed down from Bulo's back, she might have trouble getting up again. She'd been debating the issue with herself when this stranger had appeared, and the pressure from her bladder finally decided the issue.

Slinging the bow back over her shoulder, she threw her right leg up over Bulo's back and climbed down. The old horse stood patiently, his own alarm at Ferdyn's sudden appearance having vanished almost as soon as it had begun. When Adara's feet hit the ground she rocked unsteadily for a moment, feeling a burning in her thighs. Oof, she hoped she would be getting used to riding before they reached the Grandeon! She led Bulo over to the road verge and let his reins drop, giving him the okay to begin cropping the lush spring grasses. Then, finally, she turned to Ferdyn.

From down here he was even taller than she'd thought – at least four inches above her five-foot-ten. And broad with it – she didn't doubt he had the strength to swing that longsword. Had she just made an error in judgement? He was showing no signs of menace, however, just looking down at her with an expression of quiet delight. From the glint in those brown eyes, she was having a similar effect on him to what he was having on her.

Adara realized she was staring and glanced aside. Then, attempting to assume a posture of bluff casualness (though she *really, really* needed to pee!), she said "Bulo and I are headed for Grandwyl." This medium-sized city, a little west of the confluence of the Grandeon and Willough rivers, was a major river port and also the seat of the duchy of Leamarch. She saw no reason to inform Ferdyn that she was actually bound all the way to Carlienne.

"That's wonderful!" Ferdyn exclaimed, beaming at her. I think I'm in love, he thought. What a luscious piece! She seemed awfully young, though. She'd probably been in diapers around the time he'd picked up his first sword. A trip to Grandwyl might be just what was needed to charm his way into her pants, though. Mm, and nice pants they were. Leather, and stretched tight across her muscular butt and long, long legs. Shit, he was getting a boner just looking at her! Luckily his hauberk came down to mid-thigh.

Adara was looking at him questioningly, and Ferdyn hastened to go on. "Might I know your name, lovely lady?" he asked, once again pouring on the boyish charm. She looked startled.

"Um, Adara," she said. "Adara Willoughby," she added. Though that was her true birth name she had been known as Adara Selden by the people of the Pine Hill area, so calling herself Willoughby was like taking an alias. She had begun to believe that Ferdyn didn't intend to rob or rape her, but that didn't mean she trusted him much.

Ferdyn threw himself down onto one knee and seized Adara's hand, planting a tender kiss on it. "Adara!" he exclaimed. "It sings in my heart, a name as beautiful as its bearer!" Oh puhleeze, she thought, drawing her hand back hastily. Growing up in one small riverside village after another had not prepared her for such blandishments, and his words and action seemed patently false.

"If you'll excuse me, Ferdyn," Adara said. "I have business in yonder bushes and I would appreciate some privacy." Ferdyn smiled a secret smile, gave a slight bow, and turned resolutely to face the river where it flowed, slow and murky, some hundred yards to the north. "Watch out for Bulo, he bites," she added as she left – hoping that might discourage her chance-met companion from attempting to steal the horse. The elderly and patient animal did no such thing, of course.

In another minute Adara was back at the roadside, feeling much better. She was quite relieved to find Ferdyn still standing gazing off to the north, and no sign that Bulo had been disturbed in his grazing. Moving to the horse's side, she rummaged in one of the saddlebags and came up with some still-somewhat-fresh bread, cheese, a hunk of smoked sausage, and an apple. She took down one her water skins and walked over to the same oak tree from behind which Ferdyn had appeared. She might be feeling a sizzling attraction to this young adventurer, but she was damned if she was going to show it.

Ferdyn walked over and agilely lowered himself to sit tailor-fashion beside her. This put Adara in a quandary. A lifetime of lessons in courtesy demanded that she offer him some of her food, but she had not brought much extra. "Um, can I offer you some of this sausage?" she asked reluctantly. He smiled and shook his head.

"Thank you kindly for the offer, but I'm quite adequately supplied," he assured her. "I had only just finished my midday repast, reluctantly preparing for another several hours' march on foot, when you and your splendid Bulo appeared."

Splendid? Well, the old fellow was colorful enough with his splotches of black and chestnut. And he had so far proven to be a steady mount – not at all bad for a horse that had cost her nothing. Having made herself a sandwich out of the bread, cheese, and sausage, Adara sank her teeth into it and took a healthy bite. Considering she was riding and not walking, it was amazing what an appetite she'd worked up over the past several hours!

After chewing that up and swallowing it, Adara cut her eyes to her companion. "I observe," she said somewhat acerbically, "that you have not yet begun that several-hour march of which you spoke. Might I ask why?" Hmm, Ferdyn thought. This girl might be hotter than a blacksmith's forge and a decade younger than him, but she was no dummy. That only increased the attraction he felt toward her, though it also put a bit of a kink in his plans for the immediate future.

He lowered his head, then raised his eyes to her with a look of what he hoped came across as puppy-dog appeal. This had worked well with his mother a couple of decades earlier, but now that he was a large and powerful warrior it rang a little false. Nor was Adara unaware of that fact. "The thing is, uh…" Ferdyn began, "I was hoping you might be willing to let me ride along with you. I, too, am bound for Grandwyl. And your Bulo is a big fellow, easily able to carry us both."

Adara blinked and took another bite of her sandwich, giving her time to think about that while she chewed. Ride along with him? This hunk? Oh, the peril to her virtue! She smiled around her bite of bread, cheese, and meat. Peril to her virtue aside – and she'd gotten quite skilled at fending off such threats the past couple of years – traveling in company with this Ferdyn might be beneficial. Likely he possessed a lot more woodcraft than she did, might even be able to help her book passage on a river boat to Carlienne without getting cheated on the fare. And if bandits attacked them, he looked like a man who would be good in a fight. She was becoming convinced that he did not intend to rob her – he'd already had plenty of opportunities to do so, and had not taken them.

Her mouth free of food again, Adara took a pull from her water skin. "Making poor Bulo carry another couple of hundred pounds will surely make him need to eat more grain," she said. Part of the supplies gifted to her by the citizens of Pine Hill included some sacks of grain, but she hadn't felt that the horse needed them yet – going along at a fast walk with only her own slim form and the supplies on his back.

"Oh, I can pay!" Ferdyn assured her. He was eager to be taken along with her, and not having to walk the hundred-plus miles to Grandwyl was only one small reason. Adara tucked the last of the sandwich into her mouth and delicately licked her fingertips. When she had swallowed again, she turned and looked him in the eyes.

"I have no immediate need of money," she said. "If you wish to ride with me to Grandwyl you must pay me with knowledge."

"Knowledge?" Ferdyn asked, nonplussed.

"From the look of you," Adara said, brushing the crumbs from her lap and sinking her teeth into the apple, "you are a man with some skill at arms. I am embarked on a quest in which such skills would be useful. I want you to teach me how to use a sword."

Chapter 9

"Use both hands, and roll it up," Ferdyn commanded. "When it gets to the top, roll it back down again. The action will strengthen you in both directions, though obviously more as the weight comes up." They had stopped for the evening, pitching camp in a small clearing in the oak woodland some fifty feet south of the road.

"I thought I would be trained in using a sword," Adara complained. But she did as she'd been told, using both hands to rotate a small chunk of tree branch that had a short piece of rope tied to it in the center. A rather large rock, weighing more than twenty pounds, had been tied to the other end.

"Before you can wield a sword," Ferdyn explained patiently, "you must develop more strength in your arms, hands, and wrists. Trying to use a sword before you have this strength will only defeat you." Adara glanced up at him, and knew he was right. She had a goodly amount of arm strength from years of chopping wood, using a bow, and performing the other chores that life at Nanny Selden's woodland cottage had required. But she needed a lot more.

She set to the assigned task with a will, and Ferdyn nodded approvingly before he began the rest of the work involved in setting up their camp for the night. The fire had been laid, but not yet lit. During their journey after lunch Adara had surprised him by bringing down a couple of rabbits with her bow. Evidently her threat to skewer him if he made a false move had not been idle.

Adara saw her companion get out his tinderbox, preparing to light the fire, and she decided to give him a taste of what she could do if crossed. So far he'd been a gentleman, and she sensed that his training regimen was both professional and sincere; but she still didn't trust him and wanted him to realize that the consequences for betraying her could be severe.

Momentarily setting aside the device intended to strengthen her wrists, Adara stooped to the fire and silently called Salomand. In seconds the wood had flared up in a strong blaze – no tiny, carefully-nurtured spark such as one could achieve with flint and steel. Ferdyn's eyes widened, and he hung back. As Adara resumed her exercise with the stick, he began cleaning, skinning, and spitting the rabbits. But he surreptitiously eyed her as he went about his work. There was more to this girl than he had thought!

Dark had fallen, and there was a pleasurable ache in Adara's forearms as she bit the succulent meat from the rabbit bones with her teeth. Trail rations were sustaining, but there was nothing quite like sizzling hot fresh meat at the end of a long day of travel!

"Ah, that was good!" she declared, having cleaned the last of the meat from the bones. Across the fire, Ferdyn smiled at her. His initial hope of getting into her pants before they reached Grandwyl was receding, as he came to realize how formidable this young woman truly was. But he had not entirely abandoned it.

As Adara tossed the rabbit bones into the firepit, he said casually, "That was a good trick with the fire. Are you a mage, Adara?"

She grinned at him slyly. "Not a mage as men would have it," Adara admitted. "But I have my little 'tricks,' as you would call them. The powers come to my command." That was overstating the case. One might cajole the elemental spirits, and if they knew you – and what you asked of them was what they were already inclined to give – they might well answer your request. It was no sure thing. But as far as Ferdyn was to know, Adara was the mistress of all such and he would be incinerated, drowned, blown away or turned to stone at her whim.

As Adara had hoped, Ferdyn seemed to shrink back a little. Whatever plans he'd had for her had just been revised, as she'd hoped. The powerful attraction she'd felt since first meeting him had not subsided, but she still felt she needed to maintain the upper hand. Dealing with a powerful warrior a decade her senior called for some leverage, lest she be swept under.

The topics of conversation turned to other things, as the two shared the fire for a time before lying down to sleep. "Tell me something of yourself, Ferdyn," Adara said. She was truly curious to learn how a young man might become an "honest adventurer." The notion of that lifestyle had a certain appeal, though at this point in her life she was focused on the goal of finding and eliminating the person who had twice sent demons to kill those she loved.

31

He smiled at her from the far side of the fire. "I'm twenty-seven last Warming," he said. "I was born in a small town not far from Carlienne, the younger child of a cooper, and my father was called when I was seven to join King Johan's armies and drive the elven invaders from our shores."

So, he *was* almost exactly ten years older, Adara realized. Along with her recovered memories of childhood had come her birth date. She too had been born in Warming, the fourth month of the year when winter was beginning to release its icy grip. Ten years seemed like a long time – more than half her life. But still, she was drawn to him.

"Did your father survive the war?" Adara asked. It was an impertinent question, but one she really wanted the answer to.

A hint of sadness crossed his fine features and Ferdyn replied, "No. In fact, he did not live to see combat. As he and his army unit set forth for the borders of Elvany, there was a mudslide. It had been raining for weeks, and my father along with more than a dozen others were smothered in it."

Adara bit her lip. She wished, now, that she had not spoken. It was one thing for a seven-year-old boy to lose his father to a good cause, dying valiantly in a fight to save the realm. But to have him perish in a natural catastrophe... "I'm sorry," she said, her sincerity plain.

Ferdyn drew himself up. That tragedy had happened well more than half his life ago, and he was long over it. He fingered his hauberk. "This is his armor," he said. "His body was returned to us, covered in mud, and I spent weeks cleaning and restoring the armor to its original condition." She blinked at him, not knowing what to say. He grinned sheepishly, gesturing at himself. "It took a few more years before it fit, of course..."

Adara smiled at him. This was the first time since they'd met that she sensed he had let her have a glimpse of his true self. It made her feel like opening up to him as well, sharing the intimacy; but she wasn't quite ready for that. Instead, she pumped him for more information about himself.

"Was that why you decided to become an adventurer?" she asked. Another wry smile. "My older brother took over the cooperage," he explained. "He was twelve when Dad died, and he'd already begun apprenticing in the trade. But I wanted something more exciting. On a dare, I went into a supposedly haunted barrow some miles to the northeast of Carlienne."

Adara's lovely blue eyes, dark in the firelight, widened at this. "Was it really haunted?" she asked. Ghosts and wandering spirits were a fact of life – one she knew well, as there were some she could call on that would grant her favors.

"Not by anything non-corporeal," he replied. "The place was the burial site of some old warlord from a thousand years before the Unification. The local legend didn't record his name, but everyone in the area said the warlord had been buried with magical protections, wandering undead servants who slew any who broke in there attempting to rob the tomb."

Her lips curved in a sweet smile, eyes avid to hear more. She looks so good I just want to leap the fire and take her in my arms, Ferdyn thought. He still knew next to nothing about this girl who had ridden into his life, but he was beginning to get the sense that she was a kindred spirit. He saw something in her of his younger self – the enjoyment of mystery and adventure that had led him to ignore the tales and go see for himself.

Adara was hanging on his words, and Ferdyn continued the tale. "I located the barrow entrance at the bottom of a long hill," he said. "It wasn't just the old warlord buried there – I think that there'd been a big battle, and while his side were the winners a lot of his men had been killed. The place was like a long, three-storey building that had been buried to hide what it really was. And on either side of a long corridor were catacombs with mummified corpses in them, each laid out with his weapons and armor."

"Eww," Adara murmured, but her eyes were sparkling.

"It was pitch dark inside, of course," Ferdyn went on. "But I'd brought along plenty of torches. I was worried about running out of air in there, though, so I didn't linger too long."

"I guess with not much air there wouldn't be anything living down there," the girl mused aloud.

"Right you are," Ferdyn said. He'd removed his hauberk and greaves, and was lounging beside the fire in traveling leathers little different from Adara's own. "No spiders, no bats, and I'm happy to say no walking dead. At the end of the corridor, down at the bottom level, I found a big bronze door that was all carved in runes. I assume they told about the warlord and his deeds, but I doubt anyone living today can read those runes anymore."

"Surely the door was locked?" Adara asked. Ferdyn nodded. "Locked, and barred from inside," he replied. "I had brought some lockpicks with me, something I'd been practicing with for just such an opportunity, and was able to get the old lock open. But the door only budged about a quarter of an inch."

Adara held her peace, waiting to learn how he had gotten in. There would surely have been little point to this tale if he'd simply left, defeated. "Fortunately I'd brought a maul with me," Ferdyn went on. "The old tomb was built of stone laid with mortar, and a thousand years of moisture seeping in from the soil they'd buried it in had leached it to the point where it was crumbling. I just knocked a hole in the wall next to the door until I had an opening big enough to slip through."

She smiled at him. She liked this young man and his matter-of-fact approach. Most people she knew would have been too scared to enter such a place – even war veterans who had faced down hordes of armed foes. "And...?" she asked, prompting him onward.

Ferdyn reached over to where Virago was leaning up against a nearby tree, in her sheath. He drew the sword and held it up so Adara could see how the metal looked, glistening in the firelight. The tapering blade was no more than a couple of inches wide near the hilt, though it was five feet long. She had little knowledge of weapons other than the bows she'd used since the age of ten, but she could tell this was not some nobleman's "for show" sword. It had no jewels on the hilt, though there was ornamentation in the form of runes graven into the bronze. The blade itself was steel, and there were whorl patterns in the metal as if it had been beaten and folded over many times in the forging. It had the look of a weapon that had taken many lives.

Enjoying Adara's reaction, Ferdyn went on. "I can't say for sure if the guy was the warlord everyone was talking about, but it was clear he had been an important man. He had been laid out in some wicked-looking black armor, with this sword at his side. There were two other bodies in the burial chamber with him – I think those were volunteers who barred the door and then killed themselves."

The girl's eyes were big, her mouth in an "O." Once again Ferdyn was seized with the desire to take her in his arms. She was so *adorable*! But he stifled the urge. If he moved too soon, he might find himself on foot again. "Did you take the armor?" she asked, curious. Did he wear his father's old armor for sentimental reasons?

Ferdyn grinned. "I decided to show some respect for old whatsisname, and leave him his fancy armor," he said. "Actually, the guy was about five-foot-six and I didn't want to break his mummified body up to get the armor off of him. I'm not sure who would buy such a thing, anyhow. But I took the sword, this dagger, and a couple of sacks full of antique coins and jewelry. After that Mom and Raedyn stopped trying to talk me into becoming a cooper."

Adara stretched and yawned. "Thank you, Ferdyn, that was a fascinating tale. I'll bet you have a lot more of them, too. But I think it's time for me to get to sleep." He put the sword back into its scabbard, which he'd had made for it with some of the money he'd gotten from selling the jewelry in Carlienne. The original had fallen to dust.

"I don't suppose you want me to come over there and keep you warm?" he asked hopefully, and she smiled at him wryly.

"A tempting offer, I'm sure," she said, "but one I'll decline. See you in the morning."

Chapter 10

Adara woke before dawn. Ugh, she had never really "roughed it" before, and her body ached in a dozen places from sleeping on the hard ground with nothing but a thin bedroll for padding. The night had been cool, and she'd slept in the same leathers she'd had on continually since arising yesterday morning. She felt sticky and smelly.

There was enough light for her to see that the fire had died down. Ferdyn was lying in his bedroll on the far side of it, mouth open and snoring gently. Good. Being as quiet as she could, Adara hefted her pack and stepped around to the far side of a large oak. The pine woods around Nanny's place had been an exception to the usual vegetation along this stretch of the Willough.

Hastily, Adara stripped off her traveling leathers and got a woolen robe out of her pack. She slipped it on and padded barefoot out of the clearing, across the ten-foot packed-earth expanse of the road, and down a gentle slope to the banks of the river. She'd noticed yesterday as they were making camp that the river took a slight bend here, and there was a little sand beach. She'd been swimming in the Willough for as long as she could remember, and though the water was cold she felt it would be worth the chill for the refreshment a dip would bring.

Hanging her robe on a nearby willow branch, Adara bit her lip and waded out into the stream. The current was not too bad here in this little eddy and she was able to go out until she was standing in water five feet deep. The sand continued out another couple of feet and then turned to gravel.

Her nipples painfully erect, Adara lowered herself down and immersed her head. Ow, it was giving her a headache! She came up with a couple of handfuls of the medium-coarse sand, and began using it to scrub the ingrained soil from her limbs. Living outdoors was a dirty business.

She was beginning to get used to the bite of the water, and her skin was tingling all over as she turned and headed back for shore – to find Ferdyn Longblade, clad in nothing but a pair of drawers, standing there staring at her in open admiration. His gaze lingered on those pink, hard nipples and she could see from the condition of those drawers that his admiration was unfeigned!

Adara sat down hard on the stream bottom, only her dripping head above the water, a scowl on her face. "Go away!" she shouted, face flushed with embarrassment. He grinned at her, the rogue, and said "But I was planning on having a bath, too. Can't I join you? I could scrub your back..."

Yeah, with that pole between your legs no doubt, Adara thought in annoyance. Did men never think of anything else? Beneath the water, her gestures hidden and her words unheard by the man standing twelve feet away, she called Onden. The mischievous water spirit was happy to help, and a gout of water hurled itself from the river to drench Ferdyn from head to toe.

He backed away in shock, nearly losing his footing in the soft sand. "You, what...?!" he gasped, his own nipples stiffening in the chill.

"There's your bath, sir adventurer," Adara said frostily. "Now go away and give me some privacy so I can get dressed!"

His erection was already subsiding, which made him seem less threatening. But my, what a fine figure of a man he was! Despite her harsh words, Adara couldn't help drinking in the sight of those strong legs, the powerfully muscled arms and torso, smooth pale skin dusted with light brown hair. She was also enjoying his own embarrassment, as he had seemed to enjoy hers.

Ferdyn turned, defeated, and trudged back toward the campsite. As soon as he was no longer looking Adara was up and out of the river in a trice, stripping excess water from her hair and body with her fingers before putting on her robe. She was shivering uncontrollably, teeth chattering. Just maybe, she thought, late afternoon before camping for the night would be a more sensible time to bathe.

By the time Adara returned to camp the chastised Ferdyn had put on dry clothing and even managed to get the campfire blazing again. He hung an iron kettle over the flames to begin heating water for tea. As she came up he eyed her cautiously, and said nothing before she retreated to the far side of the oak tree to get dressed. At least she had some clean underwear to put on.

When Adara emerged again, hastening to stand beside the fire and get warm, Ferdyn said quietly, "I… I'm sorry I startled you. That was one of the 'powers' you mentioned?" She smiled at him to show there were no hard feelings.

"That's right," she said. "I want to learn to handle a sword because it's always good to have another skill, but I'm quite capable of taking care of myself."

Shortly he handed her a mug of tea, and she cupped it in her hands. Ah, the warmth… so good! "Mmm," she said, inhaling its aroma. "Raspberry leaf, rose hip, and… hawthorn?" He looked from where he was rummaging in his pack for some porridge grain.

"Yes, how did you know?" Adara realized she had really not told him anything all about herself. They'd spoken little during the hours they were riding together yesterday afternoon, and at the campfire she'd mostly encouraged him just to talk about himself.

"I'm an herbalist," she admitted. He grinned at her.

"Among other talents, it would seem," he said. She nodded with an answering smile.

"I don't believe you told me, Adara," Ferdyn went on as he dumped a quantity of coarsely ground wheat into a pot of boiling water, and added a pinch of salt, "why it is that you're traveling to Grandwyl?"

The man was actually feeding her breakfast out of his own stores without any prior discussion, Adara realized. Clearly he was a randy fellow and did, truly pose a threat to her virtue – but just because she couldn't trust him not to try to get into her pants didn't mean she couldn't trust him with at least a *part* of her story. "I'm actually going to Grandwyl to catch a riverboat," she admitted. "I'm headed for Carlienne."

Ferdyn gave the pot a stir, and then sat back on his haunches to sip at his own mug of tea. He smiled at her. "What a coincidence – that's exactly where I'm headed. Maybe we could save some money by sharing a cabin?" He waggled his eyebrows at her to let her know he was not serious.

Adara groaned. "*Stop*, already," she laughed. "You are a very attractive man, Ferdyn, and I have come to like you a great deal in just the short time since we met. But I am a maiden, and am planning to remain that way for the time being. It would make our journey together a lot easier if you would *not* be trying to lift my figurative skirts every hour or so."

He raised his eyebrows at that. Daughters of the nobility might possibly survive to age seventeen, or at least to marriage, without losing their maidenheads; but it was unusual among the general populace. Had not Mother Maridem commanded that women's power of creating new life be freely exercised? In some places in Tanar, including Carlienne, the Mother Cult had temples where young women could honor the goddess by offering themselves to worshipers. Such devotions were said to be a sure cure for infertility.

Ferdyn stirred the porridge again. It was almost ready, and he took the pot off the fire. As he dished it out into two wooden bowls, he remarked "It would make *my* journey easier if you'd just *let* me lift your figurative skirts…" Adara decided not to encourage him. She took the bowl of porridge with a murmur of thanks and sat blowing on it. A pity there was no milk!

An hour later, they were on the road again. This time Ferdyn sat the saddle, with Adara riding behind him. They were both hung about with weapons and packs, and it was not a comfortable ride. Oh, for a couple of real riding horses, and a pack horse bringing up the rear!

Poor Bulo didn't seem very happy about the situation. This trip was the most exercise he'd gotten in a long time, and he plodded along at a pace little faster than what they could have managed on foot. After a couple of hours of this, Adara asked to be let down. She slung her pack on the back of the saddle, and walked along beside the horse with her bow strung and ready, hoping to bag them some more fresh meat. Trail rations were all very nourishing, but at the end of a long day of travel one longed for something juicy and sizzling.

They stopped briefly at midday, filling their water skins from a spring that had been enclosed with stone not far from the road as an aid to travelers. It offered a trough full of sparkling cool water, and Bulo drank his fill as the two humans ate some trail bread and apples. Adara gave a second apple to the horse, which he seemed to appreciate.

As they made to get underway again, Adara said "Let me go ahead by a quarter mile, will you? I think I might have a better chance at game if I'm moving quietly. Old Bulo isn't exactly flannel-footed." The horse's enormous hooves were heavily shod in iron, and even on the packed earth of the river road they made a racket.

"Fine with me," Ferdyn said. He had to admit, not having to share the old fellow's back with another rider in addition to all their baggage was a boon.

Adara smiled at him and set off, a water skin at her belt along with her dagger but only her quiver of arrows at her back. Her bow, strung, was in her hand. She had no fear that Ferdyn meant to steal her old horse. Who would risk hanging for such an animal? And besides, if he were to get where he was going, he would have to pass her on the road. Ferdyn waited until Adara had gone out of sight before mounting up, sighing slightly as her lithe form vanished around a bend.

The river road here offered clear views of the river to the north, but the slopes to the south were a fairly dense woodland of oak, beech, ash, hazel and other deciduous trees. They were all vibrant green with new spring growth, and in another few weeks it would be impossible to see between them.

Adara moved along quietly on her soft boots, her senses alert for squirrels, rabbits, hares, or even perhaps deer. Dealing with butchering a deer would slow them down a bit, but it would be enough meat to last them for a few days. There were many birds stirring in the forest to her left, and a fat partridge or grouse would not go amiss, either.

These woods were very different from the pine woods she'd roamed as a child, though – much harder to see into, for one thing. She wanted to maintain a good pace, or else Ferdyn on Bulo would soon be catching her up. She'd had a hard time keeping up with him before their lunch break.

Suddenly she rounded a bend and found herself looking at a short, broad man clad in an assortment of mismatched clothing with odd bits of armor added. It appeared he'd been waiting for her – or someone – to arrive. He was carrying a crossbow, and it was cocked and pointed in her direction. "Stand and…" he began, then realized that he was addressing a young woman who did not appear to be carrying anything beside a bow.

He lowered the crossbow slightly, but there was the suggestion that it might be raised again long before she could get off a shot with her bow. An evil, partially toothless grin spread across his ugly features. The highwayman, for surely that was what he must be, appeared to be on the shady side of thirty-five, with a ragged growth of black beard clothing his cheeks. She thought that his complexion wasn't really as dark as it looked. He probably just hadn't washed in recent months.

"What have we here," he said softly, his tone insinuating. "A forest nymph?" Adara had stopped cold and was beginning to back away, her eyes wide and riveted on the bandit and his crossbow. He gestured with the weapon. "Hold it right there, missy," he said. "Just lay your bow down in the road, and then come over here. I'd hate to have to shoot a pretty piece like you, but I'll do it if you make me."

Now he was taking aim, and Adara quailed. She could call on Salomand for aid, but it was pretty likely the crossbow would still get fired. Could she jump out of the way in time? No, better to call on Nomen instead. This elemental spirit was the one she was least familiar with, the hardest to cajole and the one, even before Salomand, whose help was as likely to cause trouble for the caller as for their intended target.

Under the cover of setting her bow down Adara called the earth elemental, and she felt the rumbling as he responded to her request. She fell flat to the ground, and the earth along the stretch of road the highwayman was standing on lurched violently.

The man lost his footing, and as the crossbow wavered in his hands and pointed skyward several things happened. The earth tremor already passing, Adara scooped up her bow with one hand while rising to her feet and nocking an arrow. She aimed for the bandit's center mass, but her panicky shot went high and hit him in the face. With a strangled cry he fell forward, blood spurting from his nose and mouth.

Adara had no time to be appalled that she had apparently just killed a man, for at that moment she heard the pounding of hooves and turned to see Ferdyn, on Bulo, coming around the bend. He had somehow managed to get the old plough horse up into a gallop, and he was brandishing that businesslike longsword and charging forward. And just as she was about to tell him that it was all right, she had this, the bandit's four cohorts came out of hiding in the woods to the south of the road.

Bulo's breed was little different in size and conformation from the destriers favored by noble knights, who dressed in plate armor that cost more than a decent smallholding and amused themselves knocking each other down at tourneys when there were no wars to fight. But the training offered to a plough horse was far different from that of a destrier. As the short sword-wielding bandits appeared suddenly from among the trees, shouting and converging on the mounted warrior, Bulo screamed and reared – in panic, not fury.

Wow, Ferdyn was quite a rider, Adara realized. He kept his seat, and even appeared to be getting Bulo under control as he laid about him with his sword. That ancient steel seemed flexible, yet it cut through the bandits' mismatched armor like a dagger through cheese.

Staring open-mouthed at the miniature battle, Adara shook herself out of her paralysis as she saw one of the bandits working away around toward Bulo's rear – likely intending to hamstring him. One of them was already down, but that would still leave Ferdyn fighting three armed and armored men afoot. All of them seemed to have discounted her as a threat. They must not have seen their companion fall.

Taking more care with her shot this time, Adara put a steel-tipped broadhead arrow into the bandit's right armpit as he raised his sword, preparing to cut at the horse's legs. She didn't think she'd killed him, at least not immediately – but his sword arm was now useless and he was out of the fight.

Bulo stood between her and the remaining two bandits, and with another arrow nocked to her bow Adara began circling around to the left. Before she could line up another shot Ferdyn cut down one of the two men who were trying to come at him. His reach far exceeded theirs. Then he somehow vaulted out of the saddle to land gracefully in front of the last man standing.

Considering how quickly the odds had been shortened, this man might have been excused for making a dash for the woods. But he stood firm, circling his tall opponent and staying out of the way of that flickering blade. He was the eldest of the bandit crew, from what Adara could tell, and a look of grim determination lit his grizzled features as he struck and parried, trying to find an opening.

Adara was paralyzed again, this time not with fear and shock but with admiration at Ferdyn's skill with that blade. It may once have been the property of some long-dead warlord, but he had owned it for almost his entire adult life and clearly he had learned well how to wield it. It would have been unspeakably rude for her to step in and put an arrow into this last man, while he was in the process of taking him down.

So, she stood there watching for another two minutes as the combatants danced with their unequal weapons. At last, Ferdyn unleashed a lightning move that made Adara wonder if he'd merely been toying with the older man, running his opponent through and ending his life.

He pulled the sword out again and carefully wiped it clean on the dead bandit's cloak. The man Adara had shot in the armpit was moaning on the ground, but the rest of the gang appeared to be dead. In one smooth motion Ferdyn sheathed his weapon, then turned to Adara. His eyes were glowing. "Are you all right?" he asked, though clearly she was.

She had hung her bow behind her back, and her own eyes were dilated with excitement. "Yes, I'm…" she began, but before she could finish her sentence he had closed the distance between them and swept her into his arms. He bent her back for a deep, hard kiss, clearly stirred to passion by the fight. Adara had read that mortal peril often had that effect on people. As it had on her! She did not struggle to escape his embrace, but melted into it – his tongue in her mouth, her breath coming in gasps.

As quickly as she had succumbed to the heat of the moment, Adara got control of herself and pulled away. She and Ferdyn stood a couple of feet apart, breathing hard, staring at each other. A part of her just wanted to tell him, "Take me right here in the road next to these dead bandits!" Fortunately, it was not the part that was in control.

Bulo had run off a few steps but was now cropping the tall grass between the road and the riverside. "I can't believe you got him into a gallop!" Adara exclaimed, breaking the mood. It had been close… "How did you know the bandits were here, anyhow?" she went on.

He smiled at her, heaving a sigh. "I didn't have any idea there were bandits until I got here," he admitted. "We felt the earth tremor back there around the bend, and I just had a feeling that you might have been involved and I should get here in a hurry." He looked around at the two bandits with arrows sticking out of them. "Looks like I could have taken my time…"

"No," Adara insisted. "I'd have been dead within seconds after shooting the guy with the crossbow if you hadn't shown up. There's no way I could have held off four armed men."

"Not even with… you know?" Ferdyn asked, making a hand gesture similar to what she'd used to call Salomand for lighting their fire the previous night. She lowered her eyes.

"Well, maybe… but I'm still glad you came!" She stepped forward and gave him a sisterly hug, and a kiss on the cheek.

They turned their attention to the wounded man, who had blood on his lips and seemed to be having trouble breathing. "I think you got him in the lung," Ferdyn said, after examining the arrow that had sunk several inches into the man's chest cavity. "Give… gimme mercy," the bandit begged, eyes glazed and pleading. Adara looked away as Ferdyn used his dagger to cut the man's throat.

"Yaelos grant him peace," he murmured as he cleaned the blade on the corpse's tunic. The trickster, younger son of Father Baldor and Mother Maridem, was considered the patron god of thieves, rogues, and others on the wrong side of the law.

Adara surveyed the carnage, five bodies littering the road. "What do we do now?" she asked. She was feeling surprised that killing one man and nearly killing another had not hit her harder. She had no moral qualms about killing them – they would certainly have raped her, and likely killed her once they'd tired of that sport – and apparently that meant it was all right to have killed them. A very strange thing to learn about oneself, she mused.

"Why, we check the bodies for valuables, then dump them in the woods for the bears, wolves, and wildcats of course," Ferdyn replied cheerily. She smiled a little grimly at him.

"You're the expert," she said. "I think I'll check Bulo and make sure he's all right."

In fact, he was *not* all right. In trying to get at his rider, one of more of the bandits had inflicted several little sword cuts on the old fellow's shaggy hide. None of them was very deep or serious, none needed stitches. But they'd have to be seen to. Adara pulled her pack down off of Bulo's back, and rummaged in it for her first aid kit. By the time Ferdyn returned from hauling the bandit's bodies into the woods, all of the cuts had been cleaned and a salve applied that would speed healing and halt infection in its tracks.

The salve stopped pain, too, and Bulo was quite happily chowing down on the roadside grass as Ferdyn came up beside them. Adara smiled brilliantly at him. "Any good loot?" she asked cheerfully, and the adventurer felt a throb down through his core. He *must have* this woman! But how was he to get past her resistance? She'd nearly cracked there in the aftermath of the battle, but it might be a little inconvenient coming up with a steady stream of armed foes to get her blood up. At least he knew now that she could be passionate as well as hardheaded, competent, valiant, and just a little bit spooky. His hopes had been raised.

Ferdyn brandished a coin purse and poured its contents out into his palm. "Share and share alike," he said, counting out half the money (a mix of silver, coppers, and a handful of gold marks). Adara's eyes got wide. Even her share, just half the money the bandits had on them – and all probably stolen from murdered travelers along this very road – was more than she'd been given to carry her on the journey to Carlienne. With this, she could afford some luxuries – maybe even buy herself a sword! Once Ferdyn fulfilled his obligation to teach her how to use one, of course.

Ferdyn grinned at her. Oh, Adara was *so* a woman after his own heart! Or she would be, after he'd succeeded in corrupting her a little more. That "no sex" thing, for instance, would definitely need to change. "And then there's this," he said, holding out the sword that the last bandit to fall had been carrying. "The rest of their weapons were shit, but this is a pretty decent bastard sword."

Adara's big blue eyes looked a question at him, and he explained. "It's longer than a short sword, but shorter than a longsword. You're a tall woman, so you could probably learn to handle something like this. And the bigger the sword you can use, the likelier you'll be to defeat your enemies." He proffered it.

"Without setting them on fire, first?" she asked with a grin, taking it and hefting it in her hand. She was already strong enough to hold it up, but she could tell she'd need to do more of those exercises before she'd be able to wield it with anything like the grace Ferdyn had shown with his Virago.

"I thought you said share and share alike?" Adara asked. This sword must certainly be worth some money. Ferdyn reached into his pocket and drew out a heavy gold man's ring, carved in runes that weren't that dissimilar from the ones on Virago's hilt. A cabochon ruby surmounted it, gleaming in the afternoon sunshine. "I suppose that's a fair distribution," she said, then added "Was there a scabbard or something with this?" It was a little long to be worn at the waist, so she'd probably have to rig something to let it hang behind her back. Which was going to interfere with her bow...

The afternoon was wearing on. After Ferdyn had adjusted the straps on the harness worn by the man they guessed had been the bandit leader so that Adara could carry her new weapon hands free, they decided to lead Bulo a few more miles down the road – away from the stink of death – before camping for the night.

Chapter 11

The weather had been astonishingly clement for this time of year when Adara had embarked on her journey; but the day after they had killed the bandits a cold rain began falling. The two of them rode miserably, huddled under their cloaks, as Bulo plodded slowly along in the mud with his head down. They spoke little, their spirits dampened.

At about the time the uniformly gray skies began to darken toward the east, they began looking for a sheltered place to camp for the night. As they approached the confluence of the Willough with the Grandeon, the land to their left rose more steeply. For nearly fifty miles east of the confluence, it formed a wedge-shaped rocky peninsula, forested on its northern and southern slopes.

The only areas that were reasonably flat for camping on were within a few dozen yards of the road, where the trees grew further apart; so they climbed down from the horse's back and began doing what they could to set up camp. Fortunately their packs had been protected by Adara's oilskin cloak, and the contents were dry.

Ferdyn held up his arms to Adara and helped her climb down. Three days on horseback had not yet inured her to the stiffness of riding for many hours a day. Then, with an encouraging smile, he got their packs down off of Bulo's back and from his dug out a fairly large canvas tarpaulin with ropes attached to its corners.

As Adara set about getting Bulo unsaddled and filled a nosebag for him to have some oats, Ferdyn quickly rigged the tarpaulin between some trees to shelter an area maybe ten by twelve feet in size. Then he began gathering wood for a fire.

It was so nice having someone this competent around, Adara thought as she gave Bulo a pat and left him to his meal. They hadn't bothered hobbling the horse during the night, and he never wandered far. Ferdyn looked up from his fire-setting as Adara joined him under the shelter of the tarp. "Think you can get this going?" he asked hopefully. He'd tried to gather wood from sheltered areas, and it was superficially damp but not soaked through. Salomand was happy to answer her request, and in minutes they had a cheerful blaze.

Still wearing his water-resistant cloak, Ferdyn carried his largest cooking pot down to the river. It was in spate and looking a little turbid, but he figured if they boiled the water long enough it would be safe to consume – and they'd encountered no clear springs during the day's sodden ride.

So far Ferdyn had done all the cooking on their trip together, and Adara wasn't raising any objections. Nanny had taught her to cook, of course, a skill she felt every person should own; but the peculiarities of cooking while camped in the wilderness were not something the girl had yet mastered. She was following what Ferdyn did with great interest, though. And not just because it was so much fun watching him bend over the campfire in those tight leather pants.

There was a fallen log lying within their shelter, a pace from where Ferdyn had laid the fire; and Adara took off her cloak and laid it wet-side down on the log. Then she eased herself down onto the far-from-soft seat. Ahh! After getting the pot set up over the fire to begin heating Ferdyn shed his own cloak, hanging it on a convenient branch stub, and joined her on the log. They sighed in unison.

"Ugh," Adara remarked. "I have got to say, the life of a bold adventurer is a lot more fun in nice weather." Ferdyn grinned down at her.

"You've hit the nail on the head," he admitted. "But I keep coming back for more. What about you? When you've completed your business in Carlienne, will you go scampering back home?"

Adara had still not told him any details of her quest, but she suddenly realized that she had come to trust Ferdyn completely. It was clear he was hot for her body, but he had not attempted to rape her. He'd handed over half the proceeds of the bandit takedown, when he'd been under no obligation to do so. Plus he was smart, skilled, cheerful, and kind. Why should she not tell him everything? Suppose he had information about the sender of the demon troops, information that could save her a trip to Carlienne?

Adara reached behind her and snagged her pack, where she'd set it on the damp ground behind the log. Rummaging in a side pocket, she came up with the singed and filthy scrap of surcoat she'd cut from the body of the pig-man Nanny had killed. Ferdyn watched her curiously. Was she finally about to let him in on whatever it was had sent a young girl on a several-hundred-mile trip, alone?

She unfolded the cloth and held it out. "Ferdyn, have you ever seen this device before?" she asked. It was clear he had traveled far and knew a great deal more of the world than she did. He took the cloth and held it up, searching his memory. The three-headed beast he recognized as a terzidrac, a three-headed dragon without wings. He assumed they were mythical, or at any rate he'd never seen one nor spoken with anyone who had. Most of the creatures used in heraldry were real – lions, eagles, bears, gryphons, and the ordinary one-headed dragons that laired on mountaintops and were reputed to speak the tongues of men and hoard treasure.

And that glaring eye was definitely creepy. The whole device gave Ferdyn a feeling of uneasiness, as if the owner of that eye were watching him from afar with ill intent. He hastily folded the cloth with the embroidered device face in, and handed it back to Adara. "I've never seen anything like it," he told her, "but it seems an ill thing. Where did it come from?"

As Adara told him of the attack that had orphaned her and her decade of memory loss, his warm brown eyes radiated sympathy. When she spoke of the more recent attack, only a little more than a week ago, his expression took on a hint of alarm. "So I'm going to Carlienne to find someone who can tell me who sent these pig-men, these demons," Adara summed up. She seemed to be awfully matter-of-fact about it.

Ferdyn reached out and squeezed her hands. "Suppose they catch you on the road?" he asked, envisioning a horde of creatures from another dimension sweeping down on them as they slept. Adara shook her head and unlaced the top of her leather jerkin. She spread the opening apart and held up her chin, so he could see the black necklace she wore.

The young adventurer's expression turned from concern to intrigue as he bent close to examine it. "Amazing!" he said. "I've never seen anything like it, not even in any of the ancient tombs I've explored. How came you by it?"

"Mama gave it to me the year before the attack," Adara explained. "I think that it's an artifact of magical power, and it may be what the demons were looking for. But I also think that it shields me from whoever sent them."

"Shields you?" Ferdyn asked.

"Not physically," she went on. "If I hadn't escaped out the back window eleven years ago, or if I hadn't happened to be away from the cottage when the demons came last week, they could probably have killed or captured me. But I think that whoever sent them has magical sight – I don't know, a crystal ball or something. But he or she can't see me while I'm wearing the necklace."

Ferdyn got up to add some more wood to the fire. The extra wood he'd gathered was drying nicely, sitting close by the roaring blaze beneath the shelter of the tarp. The water was boiling, as well; but he thought he'd give it a few more minutes before doing anything with it. He sat back down, musing.

"If this necklace protects you from scrying, how do you suppose the demons keep finding you?" he asked. Fingers idly running over the necklace's central gem, which felt somewhat warm to the touch, Adara considered. She'd thought about this many times over the past week. Finally she spoke.

"It took them eleven years to find me again, after I escaped them the first time. I think that whoever it is has ways of finding out where the necklace is from people who have seen it. Maybe he or she has human agents, too – people who could ask around. Or maybe the shielding effect is like a hole in his magical vision. That would be as revealing as if he could see me." Somehow, she sensed that her antagonist was male – though she could not say how she knew.

Now it was Ferdyn's turn to sit silent for a minute or two, pondering. "Perhaps," he said at last, "it's a bit of both. Your demon master, who surely must be a powerful magus, sends out his scrying spells. He finds an area where they don't work, maybe as big as a whole village and its trading area. Then he sends someone to ask around. Your mother wore that necklace before she gave it to you?"

Adara nodded. "It could be the demons who came to your family's house back then expected to find an adult woman wearing the necklace," Ferdyn said. "They might not even have known there was a child in the house." She sat, aghast at the thought. But there was never anything she could have done about it. Instead, she focused on the present situation.

"If you're right, Ferdyn, this 'Magus X' character probably won't be able to pinpoint my location as long as I'm on the move. There'd be no way for him to have a human agent scout the area to find out where I really am, and as long as I keep the necklace hidden nobody would be able to tell this agent anything anyhow."

"Unless that agent back in Pine Hill can report your description," Ferdyn pointed out. Adara shivered, and he put an arm around her and brought her up close. She put an arm around his back and hugged him gratefully. There was nothing sexual about the contact.

"Should I go in disguise?" she wondered in a small voice. Suddenly the world had begun to seem a lot more threatening.

Ferdyn squeezed her a little harder. "You'll be fine," he promised. "Between your 'powers' and my sword, who's going to defeat us?" She looked up at him in wonder. They had become "us"? Adara squeezed him back.

"You're right," she said, sitting up a little straighter. "Nobody's going to catch me before I get to Carlienne, and once I arrive I'll have a whole city full of the king's soldiers to protect me. No way a band of pig-man demons will come at me there."

He smiled down at her, pleased that his support had restored her positive attitude. "So once you find out who's after you or your necklace," he said, "what's your next move? Send him the necklace by special messenger so he'll stop chasing you?" He'd said it flippantly, but Adara still frowned up at him.

"Hardly," she said. "When I find out who it is, I'm going to track him down and kill him for murdering my parents."

Chapter 12

Adara awoke to find herself more or less in Ferdyn's arms. They were both fully clothed and wrapped in their bedrolls as well, but after a supper of trail stew they'd put their bedrolls down side-by-side near the fire. This was the first time they had not slept on opposite sides of that symbolic barrier. He was now pressed up against her from behind, his right arm draped over her body.

From the sound, the rain had stopped sometime during the night. Adara needed to empty her bladder, and she began trying to wriggle out of Ferdyn's embrace. He woke and drew her closer, pushing her hair aside and kissing the back of her neck. A little thrill ran through her. Oh, if only she didn't have to pee so badly!

"Let me up, I've gotta go!" she murmured, and he reluctantly released her. Ferdyn pulled his arms back inside the bedroll and wistfully stroked his stiff cock through the layers of cloth and leather that covered it. Mmm. Someday, Adara, he promised silently. But he needed to go, too, and had soon crawled out and put his boots on.

Praise Baldor, the day had dawned clear. Raindrops sparkled everywhere in the sunlight, and both of them felt as if a weight had been lifted from their souls. They breakfasted on trail bread, avoiding having to cook porridge or clean up after it; but it still took them more than an hour to get moving again. Even Bulo seemed to be in better spirits.

"What was that stuff you put on Bulo's wounds?" Ferdyn asked as he got the old horse saddled and loaded up with their still-damp gear. Every one of them appeared to have closed up neatly, without a trace of infection.

"It's one of Nanny Selden's secret salves," Adara replied with a smile. "She taught me how to prepare it, but I'm sworn never to reveal its ingredients to anyone except an apprentice I take for myself. I don't suppose you're thinking of becoming an herbalist?"

Ferdyn laughed. "Maybe when I'm Nanny's age," he suggested. "This adventuring life can't go on forever, and I might need something to fall back on."

"Look me up, then," she said. "In the meantime, don't forget I'm supposed to be apprenticing to you in swordsmanship!" Truth to tell, between killing off those bandits and all the cooking and so forth he'd been doing, the young adventurer had more than paid for his slow horseback ride. But Adara was really eager to learn to use the businesslike blade she now wore strapped to her back.

They mounted up, and Bulo set off down the road at a brisker pace than he'd maintained at any point during yesterday's hours-down downpour. "It's kind of hard to practice at swordsmanship while riding," Ferdyn pointed out. "And you still need to strengthen your wrists if you're going to be able to handle that bastard sword. But if it's not raining when we camp tonight I can give you a few pointers. Tomorrow we should reach Grandwyl."

A pang of regret struck Adara as she realized that this part of her journey, alone in a near wilderness with Ferdyn, would soon be over. On the plus side, they would presumably be taking passage on the same river boat, riding for days downriver to Carlienne – if *not* in the same cabin! It wasn't as if she was never going to see him again. That time wouldn't come until they'd landed at the docks on Carlienne Bay, and gone their separate ways. Another pang.

The day remained dry, if breezy and with frequent scudding clouds obscuring the sun. Yesterday's rain seemed to have enlivened the forest, and the grass at the road's verges was growing almost before their eyes while wildflowers arose and blossomed. The companions talked more today, idle chitchat or more tales of Ferdyn's adventures.

At midday they stopped, watering Bulo from the nearby river. The Willough was now twice the width it had been near Pine Hill. "Let's try having you ride in front again," Ferdyn suggested after they'd relieved themselves and eaten some trail bread for lunch. They rearranged the baggage so that it was all tied to the rear of the saddle, resting on the horse's capacious rump; while Ferdyn sat slightly back in the saddle and Adara squeezed in front of him. With her bow hung from the front of the saddle on one side and the quiver of arrows (along with her sword) hung on the other, she was now in a position to spot, and shoot, any small game that might be within range. They hadn't had any fresh meat in a couple of nights.

Ferdyn had his feet in the stirrups, which left Adara with nothing but her sense of balance to keep her upright on the saddle. They rounded a bend and Adara found herself locked eye to eye with an enormous hare. He appeared to have just come up from drinking at the river, and froze when the horse and its riders appeared.

Instantly, she grabbed an arrow with her left hand and the bow with her right. The lagomorph panicked and took off like a shot across the road, heading for the woods up to their left. Adara tracked him, and as soon as Bulo's head and neck were not in the way she fired – and nearly fell off the horse. In an instant Ferdyn's strong arms were around her waist, keeping her in the saddle. "You got him!" he said cheerfully. She turned her head and grinned back at him, and he planted a kiss on her cheek. Then he climbed down and retrieved the hare.

Minutes later the dead animal had gone into a game bag and joined the mountain of their belongings that bobbed atop Bulo's rump, and they were on their way again. Though Adara was in no danger of falling off at the moment, Ferdyn slipped his arms around her again and pressed his nose into her hair.

After days of living rough since her last real bath, it certainly did not smell of perfume. But he loved the way it smelled, the fine and silken texture of it, he… loved. Ferdyn sat back up in the saddle, astounded at the revelation. This lanky young woman, so different from his society's notions of a proper consort, had completely captured his heart!

They caught no further prey this day, but the hare was big enough to feed them both. The ridge above the road was so steep now that they were forced to camp beside the river, in what little shelter a clump of willows could offer. While Ferdyn laid the fire and prepared to spit the hare, Adara wandered out with her dagger and harvested some of the plants she'd noticed in the vicinity. She took some willow bark, some yarrow stalks, and harvested all the leaves from a motherwort plant she found growing beside the road. She hadn't really admitted to herself why she wanted it, but she took it anyway.

The herbs leaned up against a driftwood log, drying by the heat of the fire, as Adara sat on her bedroll, laid on the soft silt atop her oilskin cloak to ward off the dampness, and gazed at the hare roasting above the coals. The smell was driving her crazy!

Ferdyn returned from a nearby spring with a double armload of filled water skins, and put a pot on the fire beside the spit to heat water for tea. Then, without asking permission, he sat down beside her and put an arm across her shoulders. Adara made no attempt to draw away. At some time in the past forty-eight hours, she had begun to accept that Ferdyn was her ally, her friend.

"Today sure beat the pants off yesterday," he remarked casually.

"Amen to that," she replied. "I'm afraid the appeal of the Great Outdoors drops sharply with the temperature, at least for me." He gave her an affectionate squeeze.

"That hare smells absolutely fantastic!" Ferdyn said, and got up for a moment to turn the spit. Both of them were staring at it as if hypnotized.

Adara was pensive. After a minute or two of silence, she asked "We'll reach Grandwyl tomorrow, you said?"

"That's right," he said softly. "This road joins with one that runs along the north shore of the Grandeon right where the two rivers come together. But about a mile this side of the point, there's a bridge to cross the Willough. Grandwyl's north of the Grandeon, of course, being the capital of Leamarch."

"The duke's palace is there?" Adara asked. Like any young girl, she'd once been fascinated by tales of kings and queens, princesses, and the rest of the nobility. But the prominent people in Willoughby, where she'd been born, and Pine Hill, where she'd grown to near adulthood, had been wealthy merchants and landowners. The largest, fanciest building she could remember seeing was the Loggers' Rest inn.

"It's a little north of town, on a hill overlooking the river," Ferdyn explained. "I've been there once, collecting the bounty on a gang of river pirates who'd been harassing shipping along the Grandeon west of Grandwyl." Adara's beautiful blue eyes were wide as she looked up at him.

"Pirates? Seriously?" Ferdyn grinned at her.

"They weren't much," he said deprecatingly. "Just an extra-large bandit gang with boats, really. They were encamped on the shores of a small tributary creek north of the river, and they'd come out at night with their little boats looking for river traders anchored along the shore. They'd take down the guards with arrow fire, then come aboard and rob everyone before disabling the riverboats' rudders and casting them adrift on the current."

Adara had some experience of rivers and boats, having lived along the banks of the Willough her entire life. But there were no large ships plying that little stream. "How did you take them down?" she asked. Ferdyn was one hell of a warrior from what she'd seen, but he was only one man.

He rose and poked a fork into the sizzling hare, then removed the spit from the fire and set their meal to cool on a wooden trencher for a few minutes while he made the tea. Adara surreptitiously added a few leaves of motherwort to her own mug. Better safe than sorry, she thought. She was beginning to get the idea that her "virtue" didn't stand a snowball's chance in hell, around this man beside her.

The tale was halted for several minutes as the two hungry travelers each tucked into half the roasted hare. The meat was tough and lean, of course – no game animals except maybe a bear would have any fat on them at this season – but it tasted wonderful after days of eating nothing but trail bread.

As they were both licking their fingers Ferdyn took up the story again. "I scouted for days until I found their camp," he said. "Had to check up half a dozen creeks feeding into the Grandeon west of Grandwyl. But once I'd found them, I waited until early morning when they were all asleep. They had three wooden longboats pulled up on the banks, and I cut them loose and towed them downstream. Fortunately it was summer, or I might have frozen to death."

Adara eyed him suspiciously. So far, his tales had had the ring of truth. But this one seemed a little far-fetched. He caught her glance. "No, really!" he protested with a smile, "I just tied the rope on the bow of one to a cleat on the stern of another, and led them back down the creek in a line like ducklings. When I got to the river I shoved them out into the current, and they were out of sight in a few minutes."

"And then?" she asked, smiling into her mug of hot tea. "I went back up to the pirate encampment and waited for people to start stirring. I had a bow with me, and I'm not a bad shot. I took three of them down while they were milling around in confusion after discovering their boats gone. Then I vanished back into the brush. They sent a party out after me, but I ambushed them. And so forth. It took three days before the last few of them just pulled up stakes and left heading north."

"So," Adara said musingly, "you didn't actually eliminate the whole band?" Ferdyn smiled, that boyish grin that set her heart aflutter.

"I stopped them from preying on the river traffic, and that was the point of the bounty. I told the duke's steward what I'd done, and he was more than pleased to hand over the gold along with the thanks of the people of Rivermarch. Everyone was happy but the pirates."

Tsk! Am I really chiding him for not being a more thorough murderer? Adara asked herself, shaking her head. The sweet girl she'd been a year ago seemed like someone she hardly knew. At least, the tale had done much to lift her out of the brooding anxiety she'd been feeling about reaching the end of their journey.

"What about my swordsmanship lesson?" Adara asked.

"Right!" Ferdyn said, jumping to his feet. He strolled out onto the beach, looking for some likely pieces of driftwood, and within a few minutes he'd used his dagger to carve them a couple of wooden swords. They weren't quite the right size, weight, or balance; and they had no hilt guards. But they'd do for the first lesson.

There was some smooth, hard-packed silt along the water's edge near their campsite – good footing for the exercise. Ferdyn stood behind Adara, holding her right arm in the correct position as he showed her how to grip the sword and how to move it. "Pronate, supinate... see?" He stepped back. "Now, practice going between pronate and supinate, and as you do step forward and back, like this. Swordsmanship is as much about footwork as it is your arm and the blade it's holding."

Holding his own wooden sword, Ferdyn demonstrated the motions he wanted Adara to copy, and she soon fell into a rhythm. She was naturally graceful, he saw, and seemed to have some athletic aptitude. Within a couple of minutes she was moving smoothly and maintaining the grip he'd taught her.

"Good, you're doing great!" he said with enthusiasm. He took up a stance facing her, and walked through a slow-motion lunge. "Do like that, lunge at me slowly, and I'll show you how to parry." Adara, eyes sparkling, leapt to the task. This was fun! After she'd watched Ferdyn parry her lunge a few times he lunged at her and she tried it. By the time it was getting too dark for them to continue, Adara was breathing hard and laughing with excitement.

"Thank you, Ferdyn!" she enthused. "I really feel like I made some progress." Then she recalled that tomorrow, their journey together would be over. She hung her head, wooden sword drooping down to rest on the riverbank. "I guess that will be the only lesson though, huh? It was just supposed to be in payment for letting you ride with me…" She gazed up into his eyes.

Dropping his wooden sword, Ferdyn closed the distance between them. "But I'll have days to teach you on our boat ride to Carlienne," he said. "At the rate you're picking this up, you'll actually be able to use that bastard sword by the time we get there!" She was somewhat cheered by this offer, but it hadn't completely wiped away her sadness.

"And when we get to Carlienne, I'll go seek out someone with knowledge of magic users and find out who that device belongs to," Adara said. "And you'll go off to do whatever it was you were going to do… And we'll never see each other again." She let her own wooden sword fall to the ground, and stood there looking woebegone. Ferdyn seized her hands in his and looked into her eyes.

"I was just going to visit with my family in King's Crossing and buy another horse before setting out on my next adventure," he said. She nodded sadly, struggling not to cry.

"Adara," Ferdyn said softly, his mouth only inches from her ear and his arms going around her shoulders. "I want *you* to be my next adventure." She pulled away a little to search his face.

"You want…"

"I want to champion your cause and fight at your side!" he declared enthusiastically. "I'll help you find out who killed your family, and we can track him down and kill him together. I… I love you, Adara, and I don't want to lose you."

She stared at him in astonishment. There was none of the jaunty teasing of his many attempts to lure her into his bed, here. He was sincere! Joy lighting her features, she threw her arms around his neck and planted a deep kiss on his lips. He held her tight in his own arms, his tongue pushing into her mouth. Oh! It was a strange sensation, but she liked it. She yielded to him, not trying to break away, as she felt his hardness pressed up against her belly and his hands on her buttocks, pulling them still closer together.

"Adara," he moaned, as dusk closed around them, "I want you so badly! Please, let us be together!" Panting, she pulled away then. Too soon!

"I can't," she gasped. "Not yet. I want you too, but I can't go chasing Magus X with a baby in my belly. Besides, I would prefer to come to your bed – a real bed, with sheets and a mattress – after a hot bath!"

Ferdyn squeezed her tightly to him, planting a kiss on the top of her head. He sighed, cock throbbing in frustration. "I can't really argue with that," he said forlornly. She hugged him back.

Chapter 13

"There it is, the famous Willough bridge," Ferdyn said with a grand gesture. Adara goggled. The little Willough, the river that had been her constant companion from birth, had grown to a quarter of a mile wide here only a mile from its terminus. And spanning it for the full quarter mile and a hundred yards on either side, was a magnificent stone bridge twenty feet wide, held well above the roiling waters by a series of arches. From the side, in the mid-morning sunlight, it gleamed like the gateway to paradise.

"Wow," Adara said in hushed tones. She was riding ahead of Ferdyn again, and he had his arms wrapped around her waist. "When was this built?" she asked. In addition to herb craft and healing, and the techniques for obtaining the aid of elemental spirits, Nanny Selden had tutored young Adara in reading and writing, cooking, sewing, and basic mathematics. But there'd been little of history or geography in the curriculum. Until Ferdyn had mentioned this bridge a few days ago, she'd had no idea such a thing existed.

"Around a hundred and fifty years ago," he replied. History was of crucial interest to an adventurer like Ferdyn. It told you where the people with the really good grave goods were buried. "King Johan the Ninth was the son of the daughter of the Duke of Leamarch," he explained. "When he took the throne his first cousin was duke here, and they were close. The duke talked him into using funds from the kingdom's treasury to build a permanent bridge. It facilitated land travel along the course of the Grandeon, and while it was being built it kept a lot of Leamarch stonemasons employed. Quite a project."

"Sounds like it probably benefitted Leamarch more than the kingdom at large," Adara remarked, as they rode off of the unpaved river road and onto the stone pavement leading to the bridge. Off to the west, they could see a large wagon pulled by a team of oxen coming toward them.

"Perhaps so," Ferdyn admitted. "But the whole kingdom benefits in the end. Johan's grandson Adalbert found it really handy for getting troops north from Rivermarch during the Nordstan War."

Adara was impressed by Ferdyn's seeming effortless command of a subject she knew little about, but she didn't say anything. She made an effort to kick Bulo up into a trot on the stones of the bridge, but only managed to nudge him into a somewhat faster walk.

Inside, she was simmering with an effervescent blend of excitement, happiness, and anxiety. Ferdyn said he loved her, and she believed him. She thought she might love him, too, but hadn't known him long enough to be certain. Certainly she desired him, and that was where the anxiety came in. She thought she was ready, finally, to surrender her maidenhead. But how long would it take for the motherwort to provide protection?

There were other herbs she could take that would put an end to an unwanted pregnancy if taken as soon as the first period was missed. But she, like most people in her culture, believed that a child's soul entered the body soon after conception. Would it be fair to send such an infant soul back to Mother Maridem before it had even had a chance to experience life? The Mother might well look with disfavor on such an act, in fact theoretically She disapproved of any attempt to interfere with procreation. But herb wives throughout Tanar did just that. What use to bring children into the world if you could not put food in their bellies and a roof over their heads?

While Adara was lost in her theological musings the clattering ceased, as Bulo cleared the stones of the bridge and followed the road along a broad curve to the left. The countryside hereabouts was quite different from the peninsula along which she and Ferdyn had been traveling the past few days. There were clumps of woodland here and there, but mostly it was gently rolling hills and cultivated fields as far as the eye could see.

She shook herself out of her reverie and looked around. "So this is Leamarch, huh?" she asked. Ferdyn squeezed her a little tighter.

"From here west along the Grandeon for three hundred miles and north from its north shore for nearly two hundred – all the way up to the border with Nordstan." That was a lot bigger than little Rivermarch, where Adara had spent all of her life so far.

"How much further to Grandwyl, then?" "Only a little more than ten miles," he assured her. "We should be there by lunchtime."

The road running a mile north of the Grandeon became paved before they'd ridden five miles from the Willough Bridge, and the travelers began to see a lot of local traffic – mostly farm carts or peddlers, but some mounted duchy soldiers and people on foot as well. As they approached the walls of Grandwyl, they had to slow to a crawling pace. Bulo didn't appear to mind.

Adara had never seen a walled city before. The capital of Rivermarch was on the Grandeon, a hundred miles east of Grandwyl – and most of that hilly, water-bound duchy was rural. But the view to the south as the road drew near the river was even more amazing!

She guided Bulo off the side of the road and just stood gaping. Even here, a quarter of a mile from the city gates, the riverside was built up. There were docks, fishermen's shacks, and little skiffs plying the shallows. And beyond those, the mighty Grandeon flowed in its steady and majestic pace – a mile wide, and dotted with what seemed like dozens of boats large and small.

Smiling, pleased to share Adara's first sight of the Grandeon with her, Ferdyn leaned forward and gave her another squeeze. "It's something else, isn't it?" he asked softly. She turned to him, a huge grin on her face.

"I thought I grew up on a *river*!" she said in awed tones.

"Wait'll we get to Carlienne," he told her. "The river's a couple of miles wide, and then it opens out into Carlienne Bay where it flows into the Westwater. That's twenty miles across, north to south, and around twelve wide."

"I can hardly wait to see it," Adara said, and urged Bulo back onto the road. Seeing the walls she'd half expected there to be a bottleneck at the gate through which the river road ran. But the gates stood wide open, and while there were guards manning them they just kept an eye on traffic going in and out.

They hadn't stopped for lunch, anxious to reach their destination, and now Adara's stomach was rumbling mightily. The river road widened slightly as it ran along the waterfront, and here many of the piers were stone instead of wood. The landward side was lined with establishments serving the river trade: taverns, inns, the warehouses of trading firms, chandleries and stables.

"Where should we go?" Adara asked. She'd felt reasonably competent while they were on the road together, even though Ferdyn clearly had more woodcraft than she did. But she had never set foot in a town larger than Pine Hill, and she felt utterly lost.

Demon Bringer

"We'll need to take lodging at an inn while we look for a river boat to take us to Carlienne," Ferdyn said quietly in her ear. "Do you want to bring Bulo with us?" Adara steered the horse over to the side of the road, where there was a hitching rail in front of a two-story building with a sign out front that said, "The Pike and Otter." It showed a large fish and a river otter cavorting in some kind of dance.

"Is this place all right?" Adara asked, and Ferdyn squeezed her shoulder.

"For a meal or a drink, it's all right," he said. "I wouldn't sleep here, though. And we'll need to take all our stuff inside with us." Looking around at the waterfront area, she could see that there were many unsavory-looking characters about. And some young women who were rather indecently dressed by the standards of Pine Hill.

They stripped their packs off of Bulo after hitching him to the rail, and went inside. The food on the fire proved to be a fairly decent fish chowder rich in cream and potatoes, with some carrots and peas added. They ate large bowls of the stuff, with crusty fresh-baked bread, and washed it down with a couple of pints of ale. Adara found it all delicious.

After their mouths were free for talking, Adara sat back in her chair and set her mug on the table. "Poor Bulo!" she said. "He's really not much of a mount, and if I'm going questing after Magus X I'm going to need a better one. It hardly seems worth paying for him to be hauled all the way to Carlienne, when I'm going to have to sell him or give him away anyhow. But I don't want him to end up as glue or dog-meat. The old fellow still has a few good years left in him."

"I think I can take care of that for you," Ferdyn said. They tossed a couple of shillings down for the meal and drinks, and went back out into the street. Nobody had solved their problem by stealing the old horse in their absence. "Come on, let's walk," he said, taking Bulo's reins and leading him along the broad, stone-paved road toward the west. They had not gotten very far when the road opened up on a broad square. Farm carts and wagons were parked all over the place, and little permanent booths were set up around the perimeter.

63

"Oh, a food market!" Adara exclaimed, delighted. In Pine Hill once a week during the season, farmers from the surrounding area would bring their goods to sell and trade in the town's main square. This was pretty much the same thing – only a hundred times as big. There were river fish year round, but this early in the season farm produce was relatively scanty – some lettuces, peas, cabbages, and other cold-season produce, for the most part. But Adara observed that some of the permanent stands offered other items for sale, as well.

She bought a little bar of scented soap from one stand, and though she was loaded down with her pack and remaining provisions, succumbed to the temptation to buy a lace shawl. She had never seen anything so pretty in her life, and couldn't resist. Ferdyn smiled indulgently at her. Those bandits' gold must be burning a hole in her pocket.

Meanwhile he was leading the horse, and scanning the farm wagons for one that would meet his criteria. Finally he spotted what he was looking for. It was a fairly good-sized wagon, probably used as a hay wain in the season, but it had only a single horse hitched to its traces.

The wagon had evidently arrived here with a mixed load of turnips, potatoes, and sugar beets – as well as a weather-beaten middle aged couple he took to the farmer and his wife, and their four children aged thirteen or fourteen down to around seven.

"Good afternoon sir," Ferdyn said politely. The farmer removed his cap and nodded to the tall, friendly-seeming but also dangerous-looking young man in his studded leather armor.

"Afternoon. How can I be helping ye?" he asked, his rustic accents plain. Ferdyn had grown up a few hours' ride from the largest city in the kingdom, and he was cosmopolitan by comparison with this farmer from the heartland. Yet the farmer was undoubtedly vastly more sophisticated than Adara was. Her naiveté only enhanced her charm, in Ferdyn's opinion.

"My companion and I have come from Rivermarch," Ferdyn told the man, "and we must now travel by boat to Carlienne. I fear we cannot bring Bulo here with us, and I am hoping to find him a new home – one where he will be cared for and valued."

Immediately the farmer took the upper hand. He grasped the horse expertly by the muzzle and peered into its mouth.

"Mayhap I could use another horse, mister," the man admitted. "But this un's on his last legs, if I'm any judge – and I am. I can't be giving you more than six shillings," he began, starting what he expected to be a long and enjoyable session of bargaining. "Sold!" Ferdyn declared with a smile. "And I'll throw in the saddle and bridle for nothing!"

The farmer looked frightened, now. "I can't take no stolen horse, you! The constables'd be on me like a duck on a water bug! You get away from me, hear?" He took two steps back. Adara stepped in.

"Please sir," she said sweetly, "I assure you the horse is mine, and he's not stolen. Bulo was gifted to me by Farmer Harling of Pine Hill in Rivermarch, so that I could make a journey to Carlienne seeking information about my long-lost parents. I just want to see him with a family who will care for him and treat him kindly."

The young woman was dressed in stained travel leathers, and tall enough to look him in the eye. But she was beautiful, and had a youthful innocence about her that convinced Farmer Brandwyn she must be telling the truth. "All right miss," he said after considering it for a moment – and pointedly *not* looking at his wife, who was taking in this exchange with a jaundiced eye. He pulled six shillings out of the leather pouch at his belt and handed them over, and shortly the travelers departed leaving the big old plough horse behind.

Tucking the money into her own pouch, Adara smiled up at Ferdyn. "I wasn't expecting to get that much," she said. "I had no idea the old fellow was so valuable. Maybe Farmer Harling was eager to see the last of me?" Ferdyn took her arm in his, as they trudged along carrying their heavy packs.

"Considering armed and armored demons keep showing up in your vicinity and randomly attacking whomever they find, that might well be a consideration," he said. Adara bit her lip. She *hoped* she was right that Magus X would not be able to pinpoint her location quickly enough to send demons after her as long as she kept moving – and kept her necklace hidden from view.

"So where are we going to stay for the night?" she asked, eager to change the subject.

"We should be able to get a room at the Duke's Head," Ferdyn said. "It's a few blocks off the waterfront and a better class of establishment, but reasonably priced." Adara eyed him sideways.

"*Two* rooms," she pointed out. He gave her a hurt look. "But… bath, bed?" he asked.

"Not yet," she replied, quivering a little inside. "I've started drinking some tea that should make it safe in a few days, but I need more doses before I can be sure you wouldn't get me with child." They turned to face each other, Adara's face so lovely Ferdyn just wanted to smother it with kisses.

"Is that your only objection, Adara?" he asked softly. She bit her lip again, losing herself in those warm brown eyes.

"Yes," she replied in a tiny voice.

With a brilliant smile, Ferdyn hugged her to him as best he could given she was wearing an enormous pack and he was doing the same. "Not to worry, dear girl," he said happily. "Your fencing master is here to show you some things we can do in that bed that will *not* get you with child. I guarantee it!"

Chapter 14

The Duke's Head proved to be the largest building Adara had ever been inside of. Its frontage covered half a block, with two entrances along the street, and it stood four stories high – all made, not of wood or stone, but of brick! Inside it was not completely dissimilar to other inns – well, *the* other inn – she had seen. There was a large, lamp-lit common room with a bar and tables where inn patrons might take a meal. Stairs led up to the rooms, and Adara was surprised to find that having a bathtub and hot water brought to the room was a perfectly normal request. Of course she had never *stayed* in an inn before, so perhaps it was perfectly normal everywhere. It certainly seemed a delightful luxury!

Adara had had her leather traveling clothes on almost continually, day and night, for nearly a week. Her desire to get out of them was nearly as strong as Ferdyn's desire to help her with that task. But after going up to the room and setting down their packs, they remained dressed and sitting in the wooden chairs beside a small round table until the tub and hot water had been delivered. The room was on the second floor and spacious, with a good-sized bed and a pair of nightstands as well as the table, and a bench on which they could set their packs. It was fully half the size of Nanny Selden's entire cottage.

Adara was growing increasingly nervous, and her anxiety was only heightened when two young men and a horde of young women arrived to set up the bath. They positioned the copper tub, which was around four feet long and a couple of feet high, in the center of a rag rug that sat before the room's small fireplace. A fire had been laid but not lit, as the day was reasonably warm.

Soon the staff trooped out, leaving behind the copper tub full of steaming water. Adara bolted to her feet and stepped over to put her hand into it. Ooh, it was hot! But it would cool soon enough. Now, she was going to have to take off her clothes. In front of a man. A handsome, charming, sexy man, who was going to show her what else a man and a woman could do in bed, something that would not lead to babies.

As the apprentice to the town's only healer, Adara had received a basic education in the mechanics of sex. The man inserted his penis into the woman's vagina and deposited his seed, and if the timing was right pregnancy would result. But what was it about this rather simple and somewhat awkward-sounding activity that gave it such allure? Why did she long to just open her legs to Ferdyn? Was it love, or was it biology?

As she hesitated, unsure what to do next, Ferdyn began removing his own clothes. He had taken off his armor as soon as they'd come into the room, and now removed the linen shirt he wore beneath it. He looked at Adara tenderly. "Shall I undress you, dear?" he asked gently. She shrugged and nodded, throwing him a plangent look. He was the expert in these matters, and she was counting on him to know how to go about it. And to think that just a few days ago, she'd been afraid to trust him not to steal her horse!

Shirtless now and down to his underdrawers, Ferdyn stepped to stand beside Adara and plant a sweet, tender kiss on her forehead. He seemed calm, not in the throes of passion; but Adara noticed that once again those drawers had a "tent pole" in them. The sight of it filled her with a combination of excitement and trepidation.

After he had unlaced the top of the jerkin Adara held up her arms and he pulled it up over her head. "Sit down," he told her, gesturing toward the bed, and she obeyed him. He pulled her boots off, then her leather trousers. She hadn't been able to change her underwear in days, either, and even she could detect the ripe odor of old perspiration and horse that clung to her. How could he even want her, in such a state?

The camisole came off, and for only the second time Ferdyn caught a look at those breasts. They were high and firm, rounded… perfect. Not too big, not too small. He kissed her on the lips, caressing them gently, and Adara gasped as he brushed her nipples with his thumbs. A feeling like an electric shock ran through her from her breasts, down into her core. She felt a wetness between her legs.

"You are so beautiful," he murmured, as he undid the tie on her drawers and they fell to the floor. He took a step back, admiring her as she stood there on the carpet beside the bed with her drawers pooled around her ankles. She had curves, her slender waist expanding to gently rounded hips and lean, muscular legs. Clearly this was no delicate flower who had spent her life lounging around in parlors! Her pubic bush was as ebon and silky as the hair on her head, her skin smooth and ivory-colored where it had escaped exposure to the sun.

"T-take your drawers off," Adara commanded hesitantly. Sitting back and let someone else do everything was not what she was used to. "I want to see you," she added shyly. He smiled at her, love shining in his eyes, and undid the drawstring before slipping the drawers off and dropping them to the floor. Ugh, they were as much in need of laundering as the rest of their clothes!

Adara's eyes widened as she beheld his cock, standing up and sticking straight out. She had never seen an adult man's penis in this state, and it was a little intimidating. Could something that big, that hard, really fit inside her? But then she chided herself for being absurd. She had witnessed two childbirths, and if a woman's vagina could pass something the size of a baby's head, the organ which put that baby inside her should have no difficulty.

"Let's get into the tub, shall we?" Ferdyn suggested. It was a little small for two, but they managed it. Adara picked up the bar of soap she'd bought earlier, and brought it into the tub with them.

"Oh, this hot water feels absolutely wonderful!" she cried, sinking down until her knees were up around his armpits and her head was submerged. She soaped up her hair, then rinsed it off again while he watched in delight.

"Here, let me," he said after Adara had finished washing her hair. He took the bar of soap from her and put some on a bath sponge, then knelt between her legs and began washing her neck, her shoulders, her arms. His member was still stiff, grazing her in the belly as he worked over her upper body. She reached out tentatively and grabbed it, eliciting a groan.

Mmm, it was hotter than the rest of his body. Stiff but yielding at the same time, and the funny little loose skin part at the tip could be moved up and down, like rolling up a sweater sleeve. "Aughhh," Ferdyn moaned. He was a young man, and it had been a long time since he had had any relief.

Adara took her hand away, looking at him in concern. "Did I hurt you? I'm sorry!" He kissed her, and began sluicing water over her arms, neck, and shoulders to rinse away the soap.

"That felt wonderful," he assured her, "and I will definitely want you to do that some more in a while. But not while we're in the tub, or I fear some of my seed might find its way to you. How would you like to become a virgin mother?" That was absurd, and Adara smiled at him.

Ferdyn soaped up her breasts next, running his hands over them and gently massaging the nipples into rock hardness. Now it was Adara's turn to moan. "Oh, that makes me feel... I don't know..." He put his hand down between her legs and cupped her sex, dipping the tips of two fingers just inside and rubbing against her clit. She grasped him by his shoulders and locked her mouth on his, moaning ecstatically. "Yes, yes," she breathed.

Adara was now clean from head to toe and it was Ferdyn's turn. He needed it worse than she did, having had no opportunities to bathe or shave since leaving the bandit lair where he'd lost his horse. When both were clean, and the water was looking much the worse for wear, they climbed out of the tub and stood on the carpet, drying each other off with the towels provided by the inn.

And now for the bed... Adara turned shy again, but lay down on it as Ferdyn beckoned her to. He lay down beside her, pressing his body against hers. His erection had gone down a little as he was washing himself, but it came up rock hard again as they pressed skin to skin. He locked his mouth on hers, kissing her passionately, as his hands roamed over her rear and squeezed her buttocks. Mmm!

When Adara was gasping again, Ferdyn got a grip and pulled back. Oh, he was so close! "Lie flat on the bed and spread your legs apart," he commanded his blushing virgin lover, and she did as she was bid. Then he crawled down the bed to kneel between her legs, bending his head to her now-clean slit.

As Ferdyn's tongue began exploring her crevices Adara's eyes went wide. *This* had never been mentioned in what had passed for her sex education! Oh, it was so hot and wet down there, and what he was doing with his mouth felt so *good*! With an inarticulate cry, she put both hands on his damp head and pressed him down, raising her hips to press her vulva against his face. A wave of throbbing sensation came over her, centered in her clitoris and spreading out to engulf her torso, her face, her legs. She quivered all over, crying out in ecstasy, as she experienced her first-ever orgasm.

Ferdyn stroked her hips and belly and grinned up at her from between her legs, his short beard glistening with saliva and Adara's juices. Success! He hadn't had all *that* much experience with virginal partners in the past (his own first time had been at fifteen, with a woman six years older), but he had certainly honed his skills in lovemaking.

He crawled back up the bed and resumed holding Adara to him, covering her face with kisses. "Oh, Ferdyn!" she murmured. "That was… amazing." After another moment she broke away from their embrace. "What can I do for *you*?" she asked hopefully.

Well, actually… He lay back on the bed with his head on a pillow. "You could start by doing what you were doing earlier with my cock," he suggested. She grinned impishly and seized that throbbing member in her right hand. She found the way the foreskin vanished and reappeared kind of fascinating.

Looking at the glistening and swollen head, Adara noticed a drop of clear fluid welling up. Curious, she bent and licked it off the tip. Definitely not urine. It was clearer, a little more viscous, slightly salty. Ferdyn groaned.

"Oh yeah," he urged, "do that again!" So, it was possible for her to use her mouth to pleasure him just as he had done for her! Adara was eager to return the favor.

Continuing to squeeze and stroke with her hand, she bend and ran her tongue around the purpling head. He moaned. Then she tried licking up and down the shaft. The skin was smooth, silky, and since he'd just gotten out of a bath it was clean and didn't taste like much of anything. Hmm, I wonder…

Adara, kneeling beside Ferdyn on the bed, wrapped her lips around his cock and sucked him inside her mouth. It was big, and she was pretty sure she would not be able to get it all the way inside. But she could work her lips up and down from the head to around halfway down the shaft – and he really seemed to be enjoying it a lot!

Abruptly Ferdyn reached down and gently pulled her head away. He didn't want to surprise Adara by shooting down her throat, in this her first sexual experience. "Just squeeze, all right?" he gasped. "I'm… yeah!" As she squeezed him, watching in fascination, his cock pulsed in her hand and a thick, milky fluid came spurting out. It shot far, all the way up across his belly and chest. So this was the "seed" she'd been told about!

Adara kept stroking and squeezing until it had all come out. So much! She put her forefinger into a pool of the fluid, scooping up a little, and tasted it. It didn't taste anything like milk. Slightly salty, the tiniest hint of bitterness. Actually, it reminded her most of egg white in flavor and consistency if not in color. As what passed for a chemist in her world, she was naturally curious about all substances in her environment.

"Could you fetch me one of those towels, please?" Ferdyn asked gently, and Adara climbed down off the bed to pick one up off the floor and hand it to him. He soon had the mess wiped up, and invited her back to lie in his arms. He held her close, kissing the top of her head, and sighed. "You don't know how long I've been waiting for that," he murmured.

"Longer than seventeen years?" Adara asked. He snorted in laughter.

"Let's just say it was more than long enough," he said. "I wanted you from the first moment I laid eyes on you, you on your oversized horse."

"I wanted you, too," she replied softly. "But, you know…" He squeezed her tight.

"We'll take care of that in a few days, whenever you're ready," he promised.

It was still the middle of the afternoon, and after lying abed in the afterglow for a while the pair got up and put on clean clothing. The inn had provided a canvas sack for guests who wished to take advantage of its laundry services, and they stuffed everything – underwear, stockings, even their leathers – into it and carried it downstairs with them.

Ferdyn handed the sack over to the person at the front desk, the one from whom they'd rented the room. An inn this size of course had a wash-house on the premises, as they had many, many bedlinens to keep clean. "Please have these cleaned and returned to room 217," he said. "And they can come and take away the bathtub and towels now."

"Certainly, sir," the clerk said politely. Adara was amazed at the efficiency of this exchange. Growing up in a milieu where even the wealthiest people in town did most of their chores for themselves, the idea that you could just wave money at people and they would scurry off to answer your every need was revolutionary. She tried to keep a grip on her reactions, though. She was all too aware that gawking at everything around her marked her as a country bumpkin, and it was not the image she wanted to project.

Expecting an arduous journey to Carlienne, Adara had mostly packed utilitarian garments. But she had brought one decent-looking dress, one she'd sewn for herself over the winter in anticipation of wearing it to the Spring Dance. She was wearing it now, and thought it looked pretty damn good. The inn had a good-sized mirror mounted on the wall of the hallway outside their room.

She and Ferdyn strode arm in arm, walking back toward the harbor area, and Adara felt as if she was walking on air. She was clean, dressed in clean and attractive clothing, with her lover on her arm. Spring was singing in her veins and she kept stealing glances at her companion only to find him looking back at her with that same expression of half-disbelieving delight.

Public displays of affection were disapproved of in their society, and the pair mostly kept their hands off each other. But Ferdyn couldn't help putting an arm around Adara to give her a squeeze and a kiss from time to time. She was so beautiful, and she was his! And then there was the exciting quest to come. He could hardly wait!

The river docks within the walls of Grandwyl stretched for nearly a mile, and the two walked along it talking with the pursers of the larger river vessels. This far west, nearly any large boat would have Carlienne as its ultimate destination. Returning upriver would involve oars, and it only made sense to go all the way down – selling cargo brought from upstream in Tanar's biggest marketplace – before turning around again. Thus, they had their choice of several.

"A bigger boat is better," Ferdyn told Adara after they'd investigated the first of these opportunities. "They're less vulnerable to pirates, have better food, and handle rough weather better."

"What about the price of passage?" Adara asked. "Do they also cost more?"

"Usually the cost is pretty comparable between a larger boat and a smaller one," he replied. "But if we're interested in speed, we'd do better to get on one that's making fewer stops downstream. And that *will* cost more."

"I think we can afford it," Adara opined. She still had every cent of the money Nanny had given her, and had barely dented her share of the pickings from their encounter with the bandits. They skipped the next two piers, and walked down the one after that where a broad four-masted riverboat more than two hundred feet long was moored. Half an hour, they had booked passage on the *Queen Miranda,* which would resume its journey downstream tomorrow at nine. It was expected to dock in Carlienne five days hence.

Chapter 15

Adara added her herbs to a mug of tea washing down an excellent supper at the Duke's Head after she and Ferdyn had finished sight-seeing. She added more to the tea that was served with a hearty breakfast of ham and eggs the next morning. A couple more days, she thought, and she should be protected from pregnancy. The lovemaking Ferdyn had introduced her to was exciting and pleasurable, but she sensed there was more and she was eager to experience it.

She was dressed this morning in a loose-fitting shirt and snug trousers, tucked into her traveling boots. Their traveling leathers had been returned to them smelling considerably better and cleaned of stains; but she doubted they would be needed on a five-day boat ride.

They lugged their packs down to the harbor after departing the inn (a place that would forever after hold fond memories for Adara), and were shown to their cabin aboard the *Queen Miranda* around half an hour before departure. Adara was once again sizzling with excitement, and doing her best to hide it. She had been on boats plenty of times – everything from rafts and small fishing skiffs to somewhat larger vessels that plied the waters of the Willough on local trading trips. But this riverboat was to those little craft as was a whale to a minnow!

The cabin proved cramped but adequate, roughly six by ten feet with a "double" bed around three-and-a-half feet wide, a washbasin, and some storage furniture for their belongings. The privy, which the sailors called the "head," was located down at the end of the hallway and opened straight to the river below. The door locked with a key, and before long the two of them were unencumbered and back up on deck. They strolled around, rubbernecking at the crew's activities as they finished loading stores on board and prepared to cast off.

Adara supposed that with ocean sailors such as plied the Westwater or journeyed beyond Elyrion to the lands west of the Sunset Sea, getting underway would be more of a production. But for the *Queen Miranda*, two of her crew cast off her lines while her oarsmen, situated on a deck just above the main cargo hold, rowed her out into the stream. Once she was into the current, she maintained just enough sail to keep steerage way, and they were off on their long journey to the west.

The ship had a pilot house at the front, and a complicated mechanism by which the steersman moved the rudder from the wheel more than a hundred feet distant. There were two lookouts posted at the front and a few more scattered around the sides, for navigation hazards could be rife on the Grandeon. Snags, shoals, other boats, and even river pirates posed a threat; but the crew of the *Queen Miranda* knew what they were doing.

Ferdyn leaned on the rail at the ship's bow, his arm around Adara, and squeezed her tight as they watched the murky waters roll beneath them. She looked up at him with an expression of supreme happiness on her face. It had meant more than her than she could say, to have him pledge his aid to her cause. The fierce determination with which she'd started out, confident that she was capable of handling anything, had been tempered by the realization that it was a big world out there – and she was by no means the fiercest thing in it.

After a time of just gazing out at the water, morning sun warming their backs, he turned to her and asked, "Are you ready for another lesson in swordsmanship?"

"With those wooden swords you bought yesterday, not that one?" Adara gestured to a spot a little below his waist. He grinned at her.

"Either is fine with me," Ferdyn said cheerfully. "But the former skill might be more useful for taking out those pig demons."

"Good point," she said wryly.

He had been able to buy a couple of official ashwood practice swords at an armorer's not far from the city gates. They were a matched pair, with dull edges and blunt tips. They had real grips and crossguards similar to those on Virago and the sword Adara had now named Voleur (after its unwilling donor); though neither of them much resembled the real swords in shape, weight, and balance. But it would have been insane for an unarmored novice like Adara to try sparring with real blades.

They'd been a bit distracted the past couple of days, and she had not been doing her exercises. After an hour-long practice session on the deck, Ferdyn cobbled together another stick with a rope and weight attached, and Adara was set to rolling it up and down, over and over again.

The *Queen Miranda* was primarily a cargo vessel, though she had a dozen passenger cabins. The crew usually ate together in shifts, but the passengers were free to visit the galley for a hot meal anytime between seven in the morning and eight in the evening. The pair lunched on ham and cheese sandwiches around one, and then took a little siesta in their cabin before getting out on deck again for another hour-long session of swordplay.

Panting, Ferdyn called a halt. Adara was breathing heavily and her eyes were sparkling. "You're really learning fast," he said with a grin. "If you keep this up, we'll get you some armor when we get to Carlienne and we can start getting you used to using that Voleur."

"Magus X, beware!" she declared with a wicked grin. More soberly, she added, "Or at least his pig-demon troops had better beware. I can't help but get the idea swords might not be much use against somebody who's able to call demons."

Chapter 16

Two days had passed, and the *Queen Miranda* and her passengers and crew were nearly two hundred miles west of where they'd begun. Adara and Ferdyn were getting into the slow rhythm of the journey. They had passed a few market towns along the north bank, which was the one most west-bound river traffic stayed closest to; and this afternoon they had spotted what looked like the spires of a major city to the south. But there had been no port stops.

"That's Grenier, the seat of Cornmarch," Ferdyn told Adara as they sat side by side in folding chairs sipping pewter flagons of ale after lunch. Cornmarch, Leamarch's southern counterpart, supplied most of the nutritional needs of the kingdom of Tanar – or at least most of its daily bread.

Adara sighed. "I feel like I'm seeing the world without really seeing anything," she remarked.

"I know what you mean," her lover replied. "Boat travel is a lot less exhausting than moving overland on horseback or foot and camping out in the wilderness every night, but it's an awful lot like being trapped on a very small island while everything goes past you at a distance. You can't get up close."

"On the other hand," she said, "we've been mostly just lounging around for two days and we've covered more than twice as much distance as we did back in Rivermarch on Bulo. Just three more days and we'll be in Carlienne!"

"We do have one port stop, too," Ferdyn reminded her.

"Ruhrsig, the purser said," Adara mused. "You've been there?"

He grinned at her. Though he was still well short of thirty, Ferdyn sometimes felt like a wise old greybeard around Adara. He'd grown up in a much more cosmopolitan region, but had traveled little further from home than she had, when he was her age.

"Ruhrsig proper is actually about five miles up the Reser River, though it's spread out all the way from there to the docks on the Grandeon," Ferdyn explained. "That's right near the eastern border of Leamarch, and it's big sheep-farming country. The waters of the Reser power a dozen woolen mills. Likely the *Miranda* will be picking up a few hundred bolts of cloth to sell in in Carlienne."

"I wouldn't mind buying some cloth myself," Adara mused. "I didn't pack nearly enough of the kind of clothing you would normally wear in a city. If they're taking on a load of goods, I suppose that means we'll be able to get off the boat and go into town?"

"Most likely," Ferdyn said. "I don't think it's an overnight stop though, so we can't take too much time at it."

She gave him a Look. "Really, I'd just like to get off this placid tub and do some walking around," she admitted. "Even if it's only for a couple of hours."

"Well, if your lunch has slid down enough, let's get the swords and have some practice. That'll shake you out of your ennui." Adara grinned at him and got to her feet.

An hour later, Adara felt a hundred percent better. Her face was flushed, eyes sparkling, long black hair caught back in a ponytail and stirring in the breeze off the water. She had actually gotten through Ferdyn's guard, and she was *pretty* sure that he hadn't just let her do it to boost her morale.

The crew and other passengers had gotten used to the young couple in Cabin four's twice-daily practice bouts, and no one was paying them any mind. Ferdyn stepped close and, wooden sword hanging at his side, pinned her in a one-armed embrace. He planted a firm kiss on her mouth.

"You've been taking your, uh… herbs?" he murmured in her ear, and her heart beat faster. It should have been long enough, by now. She nodded, eyes shining. "Let's take our swords back to the cabin, then, shall we?" Ferdyn said, doing a remarkable impression of a young man who had *not* just sprouted an erection.

Five minutes later they were locked into their cabin and had their clothes off. They'd been making love two or three times a day with hands and mouths, and that had been delicious. But Adara still had her maidenhead, and she was growing eager to part with it.

They knew each other's bodies well by now – the secret ticklish spots, the stroke or squeeze that would bring ecstasy. But Adara had been told by some of her peers, girls her age who'd already been married for a year or two, that breaking the hymen was a painful experience. So she was suddenly shy again with the man who had been her companion for more than a week and her lover for three days.

"I want to make you come first," Ferdyn told her gently, and had her sit on the edge of the bed and then lie back with her legs spread as he knelt on the floor beside it and pleasured her with his mouth. Adara had begun to learn how to give pleasure to herself, as well, and she fondled and tweaked her nipples and sucked on her fingers. Just this morning she had sucked him to orgasm for the first time, swallowing his hot seed, and she was beginning to find that oral stimulation enhanced the sensations during sex.

Adara cried out and shuddered, and a flood of slightly salty juices on his tongue told Ferdyn that he had been successful once again. For a girl who had held onto her virginity to the advanced age of seventeen, she had proven to have no trouble throwing herself into lovemaking with passion and enthusiasm. Now she was as hot and wet down there as it was possible for her to get, and soon it would be time.

He joined her on the bed, folding her tenderly in his arms. Then he began kissing her ears, her neck, her shoulders. He took a nipple in his mouth and sucked gently until she squealed. Taking his cock in his right hand and kneeling between her legs, Ferdyn began rubbing the head around Adara's swollen vulva, coating it with slick juices from her recent orgasm. Then he began gently pushing it inside – in a bit, out again, in a little further. The resilient, cushiony head of his cock met the resistance of her hymen and pressed against it, stretching it a little before backing off again.

The little membrane blocking her canal had a hole in it already, for the passage of vaginal secretions and menstrual fluid. His excitement tempered by concern for Adara, Ferdyn pressed forward again, a little harder – and burst through! There *was* a little twinge of pain, but Adara scarcely noticed it beside the sensation of Ferdyn's hot, hard cock filling her. Knees bent, she thrust her pelvis up to meet him. "Yes, Ferdyn, yes! I want you all the way inside!" she cried out. After that, it was all he could do to hold on for another minute.

Chapter 17

In mid-afternoon on the fifth day since leaving Grandwyl the *Queen Miranda* sailed out into Carlienne Bay, all sails aloft, and made a beeline for her home pier in Carlienne Harbor. The bay gave out onto the Westwater through a relatively narrow opening, which had been made still narrower over the millennia by the works of men. Mighty fortresses armed with the largest ballistae guarded the entrances on either side, and many said it was the best harbor to be found anywhere on the continent of Eorla.

It was a bright but breezy afternoon, and the lumbering riverboat rolled in the chop as she plowed north from the river's mouth at the best speed she could manage. Standing on deck, holding onto Ferdyn to help her keep her footing, Adara was looking a little green around the gills. Even so, her eyes were glued on the city they were approaching, and they were wide with wonder.

"Oh, Ferdyn, it's magnificent!" she said quietly, astonished at the extent of the kingdom's capital with its many tall spires. On a promontory overlooking both the bay and the Westwater was a pile of white stone she had to assume was the royal palace – home to King Arden's court and seat of the government of Tanar.

Fortunately the ship found its mooring before Adara lost the lunch she had eaten not long before they'd reached the river's mouth and entered the bay. Ferdyn, as usual, seemed unaffected. Was there no situation that could give the man pause? He had been all-knowing, all-confident since the day she had met him. Not that she was really complaining…

Loaded down with their packs that had grown still heavier thanks to their shopping excursion in Ruhrsig, the local lad and his teenage consort from the hinterlands walked down the pier and into the waterfront area. The teenage consort was trying hard not to stare open-mouthed at all she saw. There was just… so much… of everything!

They'd spent much of the previous day – that not taken up in swordplay and other sports – discussing their quest, and what they would do when they arrived. "We'll need horses right away," Ferdyn had insisted. "Carlienne is spread out, and we'll probably have to go up to the top of Kingshill to consult with the Royal Mage about your Magus X. Then whatever he tells us, I'm going to have to stop by King's Crossing to visit with Mom and Raedyn and his family before we set off on our mission to make the world safe for Willoughbys."

"I'll get to meet your mother, and your brother and his family?" Adara had asked. "Absolutely," Ferdyn promised. Mom and his elder brother had been hoping for years that Ferdyn would meet a Nice Girl and settle down, but he wondered how they would react when he brought them this lovely, innocent, and somewhat deadly young woman.

They'd probably just roll their eyes and move on, would be his guess. Ferdyn's contributions to the family coffers over the years had done much to change their attitude toward his chosen calling – given that one or two marks was a good wage for a skilled workman for a week, and he regularly brought in many times that with his adventuring. Of course, the risk of a skilled workman being killed in the performance of his job was relatively low – but we all had to die sometime.

Now they were standing on the long, curving road that fronted the harbor, and Ferdyn gestured to Adara to follow him as he set off to the right. Carlienne Bay's shape was roughly that of an oblong bowl, with the two-mile-wide mouth of the Grandeon on its eastern side and, ten miles away, the narrower opening giving out onto the Westwater. The city of Carlienne itself ran from the northern shore of the Grandeon all around the northern side of the bay to Fort Norguard on the west.

And except for an area around the docks, two or three blocks deep, all of that city was at an ever-increasing elevation. Kingshill was one of the highest, but the northern shore was ringed in little hills. They were all crusted over with buildings, here in one of the oldest cities of man on Eorla. The bay's south shore was lower, marshier, and home to half a dozen thriving small cities. Many of them had been built on landfill.

Fortunately they had not had to walk long, less than a mile, before they came to the stables that were Ferdyn's intended destination. The place was far larger than Adara had expected, spreading out to the east for more than a city block. The smell, on this warm afternoon, was… let us say, a change from fish.

They stepped into the timber-built front office and took off their packs, which hit the floor with resounding thumps. A pimply-faced lad of around fourteen was manning the front counter. "Hello, Thomas!" Ferdyn said heartily. The kid blinked.

"Ferdyn!" he said finally in recognition. "You grew a beard!"

"And you grew a couple of inches, since the last time I saw you," the young adventurer replied. "Is Daniel around?"

The kid gave a lopsided grin. "I'll go get him!" he said, and sprinted off. Adara had a moment to reflect that the "kid" was probably all of three years younger than she was. Her time spent with Ferdyn seemed to have given her a different, more adult perspective on the world.

Shortly Thomas returned with a man closer to Ferdyn's age in tow, but clearly a relation. A much-older brother, Adara decided. Daniel came around the counter and embraced Ferdyn in a bear hug. "You're still alive!" he crowed. "Did you bring Penelope back to me?"

Ferdyn's face fell. "I'm sorry," he said seriously. "She fell when I was cleaning out a den of bandits over in Rivermarch. That's why I'm here. I need a new mount for me, and one for my friend." He gestured toward Adara, who'd just been standing taking this all in. Ferdyn had all these good buddies, these old friends. But she had somehow never developed close friendships among her peers, even though she'd been a valued member of Pine Hill's community. Was there something wrong with her?

Daniel was gazing at Adara in frank appreciation. "They grow them tall in Rivermarch, it appears!" he said with a smile. "I am Daniel Hostler, at your service milady." He held out a hand, and when she took it he brought it to his lips. *Maridem save us, are they all like that?* Adara wondered.

"I'm Adara Willoughby, Ferdyn's… *special* friend," she said. The idea of Ferdyn staking out a claim as if she were as much his property as a horse held little appeal, but at the moment she was anxious to deflect any unwanted sexual attention.

Daniel, who was really kind of good-looking in a musclebound and coarse-featured kind of a way, sighed heavily. "I don't know how you do it, Ferdyn, I really don't." He sighed again. "I wish you well, then. So, you were saying you're looking for a couple of mounts?"

Ferdyn, who didn't appear to have been the slightest bit worried about Daniel's interest in Adara, smiled and said "A couple of young geldings would be good, I think. Some of the Khoureshi breed if you have any." Even Adara, in her remote riverside village, had heard of Khoureshi horses. They had supposedly originated in the Sultanate of Kouresh on the eastern side of the Crestans – medium in height, slender of build, and one of the toughest breeds of horse in the world.

Daniel gave a pained grin, and Adara revised her opinion. Perhaps he was not so much a good old friend as a long-time acquaintance, a business associate. It occurred to her that if Ferdyn had any close friends from his youth they would likely be found north of here in King's Crossing, where he'd grown up – not in the heart of the capital.

Soon they were led through a back door into the stableyard, where a dozen horses were loose and clustered around a watering trough and pile of hay. Outside the paddock fence, the yard was lined on three sides with buildings containing individual stalls. Almost every one of them was occupied.

Daniel led the way, not to one of the stalls outside the paddock, but toward the small herd gathered around the food and water. "Simdal!" he called, and a dark bay gelding lifted his head from the hay pile. He looked to be no more than six or seven years old, lean but glossy of coat and bright of eye.

He looked like a wonderful horse to Adara, but Ferdyn looked on the animal with disfavor. "Let me see a few more," he commanded, and Daniel rounded up another horse – a dapple grey – from among the herd loose in the paddock. "This is Zarhya," he said. "A mare," Ferdyn pointed out. "Geldings are stronger, and where we're going we'll need that strength."

Inasmuch as he had no idea where they were going, besides King's Crossing, Adara wondered at Ferdyn's speech. She was quite taken with the pretty mare, but had the idea that his attitude might be all about the price. And after paying for their passage downriver, and their trip into Ruhrsig, their purses were not all that fat. Better she just keep her mouth shut and learn from the master.

"These are the only two Khoureshis on the lot at the moment," Daniel said. "I've got plenty of rounceys, some coursers, four or five destriers…" Adara had no idea what a rouncey was, but apparently it was not something Ferdyn wanted to consider. She held her peace, and after close to an hour the pair of them had transferred their belongings to Simdal and Zarhya and were guiding them through the byways of Carlienne in the direction of Kingshill. And even after paying for the horses and their tack, they still had some coin in their pockets – if not a great deal of it.

Adara urged the mare forward, catching up with Ferdyn. It was getting on toward late afternoon, and she was wondering where they were going. Zarhya was a sweet mount, young and nimble, yet seemingly as biddable as old Bulo had been. She was well-pleased with the results of Ferdyn's skillful bargaining session.

"Are we going to seek audience with Magus Milegos today?" she asked. Ferdyn grinned at her. He was finding his Simdal every bit as much of a joy as she was Zarhya, and he was quite pleased with himself. He and Daniel had known each other for years, but he always seemed to get the better of him, somehow.

"It's late for that," he replied. "By the time we get up to Kingshill the offices of the Seneschal will probably be closed for the afternoon. And Cruztan Milegos is an old man. I thought we'd take lodging in the Palace District and be there first thing in the morning, hats in hand." Adara smiled winningly back at him.

"That sounds like a plan," she said. Then, putting her heels into Zarhya's flanks, she added "Race you!"

Chapter 18

Adara awoke atop the broad, cloud-soft featherbed in the King's Arms inn, several blocks down the hill from the palace, wrapped in Ferdyn's embrace. Ahh, she thought, feeling warm and peaceful and as if she didn't have a care in the world. Last night they'd had another delightful and much-needed bath together, and then gotten sticky again before lying down to sleep.

She still wondered sometimes whether her feelings for Ferdyn were truly love, or just biology. But whatever they were, they were wonderful. All she had to do was close her eyes, and her mind would be filled with images of her lover: his smiling face, warm brown eyes full of love; the muscles of his torso sliding beneath the smooth skin, his cock standing at attention just for her. Mmm.

Still, there was business to conduct this morning. Before Ferdyn could awaken and begin thinking of ways to put his morning hard-on to use, Adara wriggled out of the bed and splashed some water on her face from the basin and pitcher that had been provided with the room. Then she began considering her wardrobe.

Ferdyn's eyes popped open and he saw her in the process of getting dressed. He sighed, gave his rising cock a bit of a stroke, then climbed out of bed and pulled the chamberpot from beneath it. He put on some clean drawers, then came up behind Adara and encircled her waist, planting a warm kiss on her neck where it met her shoulder as she was deciding what to put on.

She turned in his arms and kissed him back, on the lips. "What do you think, love?" she asked. "Should I go for Warrior Woman or Proper Lady?"

"Court Magus Milegos has to be eighty if he's a day," Ferdyn replied. "When I was a kid and my grandma was still alive, she told me he'd been Court Magus to King Johan when *she* was a girl. I think he'd probably respond better to Proper Lady – even if it's only a disguise."

With a wry grin, Adara slugged him on the arm in retribution for this slur on her qualities of lady-ness – thereby proving the truth of it. In the village of Pine Hill fine ladies had been in short supply in any case, as most people of both sexes there were expected to work for a living. And living in semi-isolation in the forest cottage with Nanny Selden, a woman who'd been a Force to Be Reckoned With for most of her life, had done little to temper Adara's natural tendencies toward the unladylike.

She donned her most respectable-looking skirt and blouse, and wrapped her new lace shawl around her shoulders. The room offered a chest of drawers with a mirror atop it, and she made sure her hair was neatly combed. Not too bad… After a hasty breakfast in the inn's common room they went on foot up the hill a few blocks and were admitted to the palace grounds by a pair of well-armed royal guards.

This small public gate was where any who were not part of King Arden's court must go if they had business with the palace. This included the tradesmen who supplied food and drink to the palace, and any ordinary citizens seeking an audience with the king, the Royal Justiciar (who heard all legal issues and decided many of them himself), or the Royal Magus. Foreign dignitaries were usually admitted, by prior arrangement, through the much larger King's Gate.

The royal palace of Tanar had been built atop the site of an ancient hill fort, and though it had many modern amenities it was still a serious fortress – surrounded by stone walls both tall and thick, and protected by hundreds of royal guards. The city of Carlienne itself had outgrown its walls long since, but it had not been taken or even invested by an enemy in the nearly seven centuries since Tanar had been unified. Today's duchies had been independent kingdoms, in the distant past.

Ferdyn, who was dressed in respectable but not opulent clothing for the occasion, led Adara to the office of the Royal Seneschal. This functionary arguably had more power than did the king himself, as it was he (and those under him) who decided which petitioners received an audience, which suppliers would provide goods to the court, and so forth.

"You've been here before?" Adara asked quietly as they stepped inside. Ferdyn nodded.

"You have to see Martin Starbrook if you want to collect the bounty on outlaws taken within Kingsmarch," he explained in an undertone. They walked up the reception desk, where a young man in gold-trimmed royal livery sat with an enormous ledger book before him. The room they'd stepped into was lined with hard chairs, but as yet no one was waiting in them.

"Good morning sir, madam," the clerk said politely. "Do you have an appointment?"

"That's why we're here, um, Stefan, is it?" Ferdyn replied. The young man's face brightened.

"Ferdyn! Didn't recognize you with the beard," he said. "Here to collect another bounty?"

Ferdyn smiled at him, and once again Adara found herself in awe of her lover's abilities. Not only was he a demon with that longsword and a tiger in bed, he seemed to have a way of wrapping people around his little finger. Herself included?

"Not this time, I'm afraid," Ferdyn said. "Unless maybe Sieur Starbrook would be willing to pay me for the bandits I wiped out in Rivermarch." Stefan shook his head.

"Sorry, you'll have to see the duke's steward in Riparre for that one."

"No problem," Ferdyn went on. He gestured to Adara. "This is my friend Adara Willoughby, of Rivermarch. She has twice been attacked by bands of demons with a strange device on their surcoats."

Adara pulled the folded cloth out of the reticule she'd brought in lieu of a pack, and held it out for Stefan to see. The young man eyed it thoughtfully. "Kind of ominous-looking, isn't it?" he remarked. Looking up at Adara, and taking her in from head to toe with an appreciative glance, he asked "You say this device was worn by demons?"

"I don't know what else you could call them," Adara replied. "They were shaped like men, but short and broad with too-long arms, and their faces were like the faces of pigs with long snouts and tusks. They wore armor and carried swords and axes, and they seemed to speak among themselves in animal grunts. They killed my parents."

Stefan's eyes went wide. "How is it that you escaped, my lady?" he asked.

"I was just a little girl at the time," Adara explained. "I climbed out a window at the back of the house and ran for it. But a couple of weeks ago these demon troops found the place where I was living and attacked my foster mother, the old woman who had raised me since I was orphaned."

Now the young man's face was a mask of sympathy. "I'm so sorry," he said sincerely. "It must be terrible for you, to have lost two mothers." Adara surprised him with a wry grin.

"Oh, it wasn't my foster mother who came out the loser in *that* battle," she said. "Nanny Selden is… not your typical old lady. She killed three of them and the others fled after they realized I was not there. That's how I got this piece of surcoat, and was able to examine the demons close up. They are flesh and blood creatures, and clearly not invincible. But they are not human, and not any sort of elf I've ever heard of. What magus has the ability to command beings from other dimensions?"

Stefan rose to his feet. "I think you need to speak with Magus Milegos," he said. "Excuse me just a moment." While Ferdyn and Adara waited, still standing in front of the reception desk, the clerk stepped down the hall and vanished into one of the doors along it. A couple of minutes later he returned. "I've sent a messenger to see if Magus Milegos can see you," he told them. "The old man does little actual magic these days, of course," he confided. "But he is surely the kingdom's foremost authority on magic and magic-users. If anyone can identify the magus behind these demon attacks, it will be him."

Just then a pair of middle-aged men dressed as prosperous merchants came in, and Stefan directed them to some chairs. "Please wait," he said. "I'm sure it won't be long." Fifteen minutes later a lad of around fifteen, dressed in the same livery as Stefan, came in through the front door. "Master Cruztan has said that he will see your friends in half an hour," he reported to the clerk.

"Thank you, Giles," Stefan said. To Ferdyn and Adara he said, "Giles here will guide you to the Magus' quarters. And good luck with your quest!" he added, before turning his attention to the arrival of another petitioner.

As the couple trailed the messenger boy through the labyrinthine corridors of the palace complex, Adara murmured to Ferdyn "This is amazing! I was afraid we'd be cooling our heels for days, waiting to get an audience!"

"You don't realize how dull life can be in the royal palace, my darling," he replied *sotto voce*. "A generation since the last real war, and most of the people who work here welcome almost any excitement. Old Cruztan is probably eager for a challenge."

Giles dropped them off in an anteroom not dissimilar from the one they had just left, though it had fewer chairs in it. Surprisingly, the small desk was manned by a pretty, serious-looking young girl who looked to be no more than sixteen. "Adara and Ferdyn?" she asked, and Adara replied "That's us." A faint smile flickered across the girl's lips and she said, "Master Cruztan will see you shortly. Please take a seat."

After they'd sat down the girl went through a door behind the desk, presumably to let her master know his visitors had arrived. Adara nudged Ferdyn. "Is this royal magus something of an old goat?" she asked in a murmur. He raised an eyebrow, a corner of his mouth twitching up at the idea of an octogenarian getting frisky with his teenage office staff.

"I've never met the man, so I can't say," he replied quietly. "But he *is* a magician…"

They didn't have long to wait before the girl returned and ushered them into the room where the Royal Magus entertained visitors. Adara was hard put not to just stand there gawking, as the large and airy room was full of interesting and remarkable artifacts. Globes, apparently representing the solar system, hung from the ceiling. There were weapons and armor, presumably enchanted, on display racks here and there. The mounted skeleton of what looked like a small dragon was over near the wall in the far corner. But the most remarkable thing of all was the magus himself.

Yes, Cruztan Milegos was an old man. His hair, which flowed over his shoulders and halfway down his back, was silver. His luxuriant beard, reaching down past his waist, was white. And though he had probably once stood as tall as Ferdyn, he was now a little shorter than Adara. Yet he stood straight and unbowed, with no sign of the infirmities of age. His black eyes glittered with interest as the young couple were ushered into his presence.

The Royal Livery of Tanar was burgundy and gold, but the magus wore black. His finely tailored robe appeared to be made of velvet, and was embroidered with mystical symbols in gold thread. On his head, he wore a matching hat with a broad brim and a pointed crown, and he had in his hand a gnarled staff with a natural crystal gem of some sort mounted atop it. Adara thought that if you were to look up "Magus" in a book of lore, the picture accompanying the entry on the subject would look exactly like the man she saw before her. No doubt that was the idea.

"Thank you, Julia," the old man said kindly, and the girl went back through the door leaving them alone. "My great-granddaughter," he told them, putting paid to Adara's fantasies of magically-enhanced virility. "Please," he said, gesturing toward a corner of the room where a pair of small, elegant divans flanked a low table, "Come and be seated."

Yes, Adara realized. It appeared that the powerful magus *was* intrigued by their situation. He almost acted as if they were doing *him* a favor by coming to see him, instead of the other way around. Fortune was smiling on her! Though Ferdyn had left his armor back at their inn room he had Virago strapped to his back. Since acquiring the sword eight years before, he had been reluctant to leave it behind. He'd never had it appraised, but assumed it was worth a fortune.

As he and Adara walked ahead of their host, heading for one of the divans, Master Cruztan came up behind him. "May I see your sword, young man?" he asked, hand hovering over the blade. Ferdyn turned, surprised.

"Uh, certainly," he said, carefully pulling Virago from the scabbard he'd had crafted for her all those years ago. He held out the blade to the magus.

The old man's dark eyes were riveted on the hilt, with its ancient runes. "Yes, it is as I thought!" he breathed, running his fingers over them. Ferdyn eyed him questioningly, and Milegos looked up. "You obtained this sword from an ancient tomb?" he asked the much-younger man. Ferdyn's garb did not mark him as an adventurer, but his build and the way he carried himself did – as did this blade.

Ferdyn ducked his head. The kingdom had no laws forbidding the raiding of pre-Unification tombs, which were generally regarded to be fair game if you could get past the reputed undead guardians and magical traps that had been set to protect them. "It came from a barrow around twenty miles northeast of King's Crossing," he admitted. "Supposedly haunted, but I saw no ghosts there."

Milegos seized the sword by the hilt, holding it point downward, and closed his eyes for a moment. Then he handed it back. "The legendary longsword of Atylan," he pronounced, and gestured for his visitors to continue their progress toward the divans. As Ferdyn and Adara took seats on one, he sat in the other and leaned forward to explain.

"Atylan was a warlord who reached the peak of his powers at around 400 b.u.," the old man said. "As well as a superb warrior, he was a magus of some abilities. It was claimed that he forged that blade himself, imbuing spells within it that would make it unbreakable, and grant the wielder powers of untiring strength and swordcraft beyond what they would otherwise possess."

Ferdyn looked at the old magus, dumfounded. Was his amazing success as an adventurer due entirely to a magic sword all these years, and not to his own natural abilities and hard work? It made him feel... diminished, somehow. He shook the feeling off. Virago might be a superior tool, but she was just that. Had not the immensely powerful Atylan fallen despite possessing it? A tool was only as good as the man wielding it.

"I had no idea," he told Master Cruztan. "Were you able to detect such enchantments on the blade?" The old magus nodded.

"When you found the sword, you were not yet an expert swordsman?" he asked.

"I was nineteen, and I'd been practicing with swords for almost half my life," Ferdyn replied. "But after I acquired the longsword, a type of blade I'd never tried before, my skills improved much more quickly."

"Just so," Cruztan said. "Well, I hope you will only use it in the cause of good. These enchanted weapons have been known to turn on those who wield them, if they use them in the cause of evil.

Unless of course the weapons were enchanted with evil intent in the first place…"

He turned to Adara. "Julia mentioned you had a piece of surcoat you wished to show me, young lady?" She eagerly took the folded cloth from her reticule and handed it over. The old magus spread it out on the table that stood between them, his dark eyes widening slightly.

"This is one of the devices of Sarand Bloodspire, the so-called 'Mancer King,'" the royal magus said in worried tones. "How came you by it?" Adara explained about the pig-demons who'd twice attacked homes where she'd been living, and Cruztan nodded.

"The Swinzen," he said. "They are considered demons because they were brought here from the dimension that is their home, and because they are bound to Sarand's service by the magical arts he practices. They are less intelligent than men, but completely loyal to their master, and as he almost never leaves his fastness in the northern mountains he sends them here and there when he has errands to be accomplished. Do you have any notion of what they were after?"

Adara felt she could trust Master Cruztan. After all, King Arden and his father before him had relied on the man to serve the interests of the kingdom, and had had no complaints. She unbuttoned her high-necked blouse to reveal the black necklace she wore, coming down off the divan to kneel before the table so the old magus could get a good look at it.

His eyes widened again. He made a slight hand gesture, and Adara felt the necklace, specifically its central gem, grow warm for a moment. Ferdyn, who'd been watching, exclaimed "The black gem just lit yellow for a second!" Milegos smiled.

"It is as I thought," he said. "The spell I just cast on you should have put you to sleep on the spot, Adara. But the necklace shielded you from the spell."

"Ferdyn and I had discussed it, and concluded that was the necklace's effect," Adara supplied. "We think that this Mancer King, this Sarand Bloodspire, has magical sight but can't see me while I'm wearing the necklace. It seems likely that he's used other agents, human ones, to ask around in areas where his sight was blocked and pinpoint my location."

The old man nodded. "I believe you're right about that, my dear," he said. "How did you acquire this necklace?"

"It's been passed down in my family for generations," Adara replied. "My mother gave it to me and told me to wear it always, about a year before she was killed by the invading Swinzen."

Cruztan nodded again. "If you wouldn't mind, would you attempt to remove it now?" he asked. "I assure you, this entire wing of the palace is shielded from all magical sight." Adara nodded unsurely. Putting both hands on the seemingly continuous band near the side opposite the gem, she willed it to come apart as she had done for Nanny Selden a few weeks ago.

Adara laid the necklace, now a long sinuous band with a gem in the center of it, out on the table. Both Cruztan and Ferdyn bent close to examine it. "Well, what can you tell me about it?" she asked. The old magus picked the necklace up and tried to re-fasten it around Adara's neck, but it would not close. Tucking it under his beard and hair, he tried to fasten it around his own neck with the same result.

"Go ahead and put it back on, dear," he told Adara, and in moments the band had once again become a continuous circle around her throat. The old man nodded. He had just a couple more questions. "Your mother took it from her own neck and put it around yours when you were small?" he asked, and she nodded. "And it fit you then as it does now, growing as your neck grew larger?"

Adara's eyes widened. The necklace had just been a part of her for years, and for most of those years she'd been unable to remember a time when it had not rested around her neck. It had seemed perfectly natural that it would grow as she did — was it not a part of her body? But now, she realized that was one of its magical qualities.

"Yes," was all she said, and Cruztan was at last ready to tell her more.

"Your necklace is a Darkshield, or possibly *the* Darkshield. It dates from thousands of years ago, a product of the magical arts of the east beyond the Crestan range. It is probably only a legend, but it is said that the eastern sorceress Astrinda crafted it as protection for her daughter, who was being sought by her enemies to use as leverage against her. The wearer of this necklace is shielded from all magical harm, and from magical sight as well."

Adara put a hand to her throat, feeling the gem where it rested near her collarbone. Amazing! "The Darkshield was passed from mother to daughter down through many generations, and was sometimes the focus of plots and bitter conflicts," Cruztan went on. "But by the nature of the enchantment on it, the magic of the necklace will die if its wearer should expire, or be rendered permanently unconscious, before she can voluntarily pass it on."

"Can a man even wear it?" Adara asked. Her mother had said it had been passed through the female line, and if it had begun that way might this Mancer King be wasting his time trying to acquire it? Unless maybe he had a daughter... But the old magus nodded.

"Hundreds of years after Astrinda crafted the Darkshield, using arts long forgotten, it passed from one of her descendants to that woman's lover – a man she loved more than life itself. Thence it was passed from father to son for more generations, until it once again came to be worn by the daughter of a man who had no sons."

Adara was lost in thought for a moment. Finally she spoke, "So this Sarand Bloodspire, in order to obtain the Darkshield, must have planned to abduct whoever was wearing it and somehow convince them to voluntarily place it around his own neck." Cruztan nodded.

"Bloodspire has risen to power in the northern mountains only within the past thirty years," he said. "And the lore surrounding the Darkshield is not well known. Even I, who am probably the greatest authority on all things magical west of the Crestans, had thought it only an interesting old tale. Or at least, I had assumed that the Darkshield had long since been lost. It would only have taken one wearer waiting too long to hand it on to a successor, after all. I fear it does *not* protect you from dying of a fever, or of simple old age."

"It's astonishing he was able to find my family at all," Adara mused sadly. "He must have been searching for decades, maybe even when my grandmother was wearing it."

"That is most likely the case," the old magus replied. "And he cannot kill you to get it. I suppose he could have you physically tortured, in hopes you would give up the Darkshield to stop the pain."

Adara shuddered. She was not sure she would be able to withstand such treatment – even knowing that once she had given in, she would surely be killed. She could think of another way she might be coerced, as well. "He could just threaten someone I love," she said softly – looking at Ferdyn. "I would yield it in a heartbeat."

Cruztan didn't take her meaning, not knowing her relationship with Ferdyn. But he was alarmed at the thought. "No, you must not yield it to him!" he warned. "With such protection, Bloodspire would become unstoppable. He has carved himself a tiny kingdom in the mountainous region north of here, amid lands claimed by both Tanar and Nordstan. But were he to become immune to the spells of myself and other mages in both lands, he might well decide to expand. We could have hordes of Swinzen soldiers rampaging through the countryside, the demon bringer himself sitting on King Arden's throne!"

Adara's eyes grew wide. She had thought the situation a personal one, of concern only to her. And she had intended to seek out her "Magus X," whose true name she now knew, and put a stop to him once and for all – though Baldor knew how she, even with Ferdyn's help, could achieve that. Now, she realized, even just handing over the necklace to him was not an option.

"If this Sarand Bloodspire has taken over land belonging to the kingdom, and poses such a threat with his demon armies, why does not King Arden send troops to depose him?" Adara asked. Wasn't the king supposed to be all-powerful, especially with the backing of his magus?

Cruztan shook his head sadly. "It's not as easy as that," he said. "For one thing, the town of Kragstein and the tower fortress above it are surrounded by mountains and very hard to come at with an armed force. For another, they are an infinitesimally small part of the kingdom of Tanar – one that our kings for three generations have not even bothered to dispute with Nordstan to the point of drawing blood. As long as Sarand remains walled up within his Bloodspire he's no threat to the kingdom, and King Arden has no intention of bothering him. We could presume that in another generation Sarand will have expired of old age, and the problem will be solved."

"But he's a powerful magus!" Adara objected. "Suppose he's able to use his magical arts to extend his lifetime for a few centuries?" Cruztan shrugged his shoulders.

"If I knew of such arts, I assure you I would not be as you now see me," he said. "You could, perhaps, take passage on a ship west, remove the Darkshield, and drop it into the Sunset Sea. That would certainly prevent Sarand from getting his hands on it, and presumably it would also halt his harassment of you since he would have nothing to gain from it."

Nothing but revenge, Adara thought darkly. But she kept it to herself. She rose to her feet and extended a hand. "Thank you, Magus Milegos, you have been a great deal of help today. I appreciate all that you have told me." The old man eyed her speculatively.

"You're welcome Miss Willoughby," he said thoughtfully. "If you'll wait just a moment, there is something I'd like you to have."

As Adara and Ferdyn stood hesitating, Cruztan exited the room via a door at the back. He returned a few minutes later carrying a small object which he dropped into her hand. It was a small gold ring, intricately etched with tiny runes. "Wear this, my dear," the old man said kindly, "and you will find that the learning of anything you put your hand to will come more easily."

Adara's eyes got wide. "Will the learning persist when I'm not wearing the ring?" she asked, imagining the possibilities.

"Certainly," he replied. "The ring only increases the speed with which you can learn. But whatever you learn, it will be with you always."

"Thank you, Sieur," she said in a small voice. She slipped the ring onto the middle finger of her left hand, where it seemed to adjust itself to fit. Smiling, she planted a kiss on the old man's cheek. Then she and Ferdyn walked from the room.

Chapter 19

The whole way down the hill to the King's Arms inn, Adara was thinking and planning. She still needed Ferdyn's help, and she dared not reveal her intentions just yet. Not until her preparations were in place. Ferdyn had a lot to think about, as well, and it wasn't until they were nearly "home" that he asked, "Are we getting on a ship, then?"

"No," she answered shortly, "we're going to get me fitted for some armor. We still have enough coin for that, I hope?"

"Enough for something like mine, probably," Ferdyn replied. "That steel-studded leather was issued to all of King Johan's troops in the Elvany War, and there's a lot of it still around in reasonably good condition. You're as tall as many soldiers, if slimmer, so you should be able to get some fitted for you at not much cost. It's fairly protective, plus it's relatively lightweight and flexible."

After they'd returned to their inn room, they began gathering their belongings. Adara changed back into the trousers, shirt, and boots she'd worn on their river boat ride, which had been cleaned overnight after their arrival here. As soon as she was down to her underwear, Ferdyn was on her like a duck on a water bug. He'd found their conference with the Royal Magus unsettling to say the least, but he also feared that they might soon be running out of opportunities for intimacy.

Seemingly, they already had. Adara kissed and hugged him, but then pushed him away. "We need to get out of here before checkout time," she told him. "This place is nice, but it's far too expensive." Sighing, Ferdyn resumed loading up his pack.

"We probably ought to go to King's Crossing, then," he said. "We can put up at my brother's house for free, and there are two or three smiths in town who can likely address your armor needs. I assume you're eager to try out Cruztan's gift with your Voleur?"

Oh Ferdyn, Adara thought with an internal sigh. That mind of his was so sharp. It was going to be a problem, soon. She gave him a lopsided smile and another hug. "Am I so transparent?" she asked, and he hugged her back. Half an hour later they were once again mounted on Simdal and Zarhya, moving along the main road north at a fast trot.

As they rode, Adara's mood lightened. It was a beautiful day, Zarhya was a delightful mount with a marvelously smooth gait, and it would surely be days at least before she would have to do the thing she so very much did not want to do. Why not just enjoy herself in the meantime?

Carlienne did not end abruptly, but just sort of trailed off on its northern edge until they found themselves riding that same north road with farm fields to their right and the cliffs overlooking the Westwater to the left. Then the road veered toward the east, and there were farm fields, houses, and even the odd roadside tavern on either side of them.

"King's Crossing is not so much a village as a suburb," Ferdyn was saying as they rode along. He seemed to be oblivious to, or at least ignoring, Adara's change of outlook. "How many people live there?" she asked, making polite conversation though her heart was still somewhat troubled.

"More than ten thousand," he replied, and she was stunned. That was close to the population of Riparre, the capital of the duchy where she'd been born and raised! No wonder Ferdyn seemed so cosmopolitan when compared with her. He truly was a city boy.

They rode on, and before long came into the outskirts of King's Crossing. It had been named centuries before because it had grown up around a crossroads where one of Tanar's principle east-west highways ran. That road crossed the great north road and continued on, thirty miles west to a fishing village that had sprung up on the coast.

Large it might be by the standards of Rivermarch, but King's Crossing did have something of a small-town feel. Most buildings were of wood and not stone, no more than two storeys tall. The streets were mostly paved in cobblestones, at least those surrounding the famous crossroads. But in the outskirts, many were nothing but dirt lanes – probably a nightmare to navigate in the rain.

Ferdyn led Adara along the north road past the crossroads, then took a left turn a few hundred yards further along and took a zigzagging course that shortly fetched up beside a large wooden building like a warehouse. A fairly substantial-looking three-story brick house stood beside it. Adara eyed it in surprise, and cast a questioning look in Ferdyn's direction.

"I *have* contributed more than a little to the family coffers over the years," he admitted with a rueful grin. "But Rae's a master cooper now, and he's been able to expand the business with no assistance from me. It helps that there are three wineries in the district, as well as two breweries and a distillery." Adara's eyebrows went up. She supposed barrels were needed for many things besides alcoholic beverages, as well. Herring, for instance? But who knew making them could be so profitable?

There was a hitching rail outside, and they tied their mounts to it. Ferdyn removed his belongings from where they were strapped behind Simdal's saddle, and Adara took her cue from him and removed her own from the back of Zarhya. This area looked pretty respectable, especially by comparison with Carlienne's waterfront district, but she supposed there might be petty thieves even here.

They hauled their packs inside the open double doors of the cooperage, seeing many finished barrels stacked to one side. Inside, the large lamp-lit space had a crew of six men and boys working on barrels in various stages of completion. Ferdyn waved to them, then led the way to an office that was built in from the corner of the building overlooking the street.

He walked in through the open door, and Adara followed along. She was feeling a little nervous. There were two desks in the room, flanking the doorway. The one on the left had a small window looking out on the street, while a window on the opposite side had a view of the workroom they'd just come through.

A man who looked to be in his early thirties was sitting behind the left-hand desk, poring over what appeared to be a ledger book. He had neatly-trimmed sandy blond hair a shade darker than Ferdyn's, was clean-shaven, and was carrying a few extra pounds. He was dressed more like a banker than an artisan.

He glanced up at them, and his face immediately lit with joy at the sight of Ferdyn. He jumped to his feet and came around the desk to throw his arms around his baby brother. "Ferd! Good to see you!" he cried, slapping the taller man's back. He stood an inch or two shorter than Ferdyn, but was wider. Nor was it all fat, Adara could see. Not bad, she thought. At least he's not losing his hair…

Clearly this was Ferdyn's older brother Raedyn, owner of the family cooperage and, according to stories her lover had shared during their journey together, the father of three. He looked enough like Ferdyn that she couldn't help warming to him. "And who's this?" Raedyn asked with a twinkle in his eye, looking Adara up and down.

Ferdyn grinned back at him. He'd hoped that by now Mama and Rae would have given up on marrying him off to some local girl, or on getting him to settle down at all. He was addicted to his adventurous lifestyle, and far too young yet to pack it in. "This is Adara Willoughby," he said. "Adara, as you've no doubt figured out, this is my brother Raedyn Cooper. I've agreed to help Adara with a quest she's on, Rae. We hope you'll be able to put us up for a few days, then we'll be heading north."

Raedyn beamed at the two of them. "No problem!" he declared. "We've got plenty of room, and I'm sure Mom and Allys will be glad to have you both. We haven't seen that much of you since the house was built." Ferdyn grinned now at Adara.

"After the cooperage began doing so well and Rae and Allys were wed, they put up that three-story brick barn next door. I suppose Rae assumed they'd be having a dozen children, but so far there are only three of them."

"Why no, Ferd – we expected you to move in there with us, with *your* wife and children." He looked speculatively at Adara. "I don't suppose there's any chance that you…?" he trailed off. She smiled.

"Marry *this* rogue? I hardly think so!" she said in mock outrage, getting into the spirit of things. Inside, her heart was aching.

Chapter 20

Ferdyn and Adara were each given a small bedroom on the house's third floor. His mother, Berenice, had a small apartment of her own on the ground floor, while Raedyn and his wife Allys, along with their three young children, had their bedrooms on the floor above. Berenice proved to be a sturdy, cheerful woman in her middle fifties, whom Adara liked at once. It made her wonder what Ferdyn's late father had been like.

They spent the rest of the day of their arrival meeting people and getting settled in, having an impromptu lunch from the stores in the Cooper family's large kitchen, and a fine supper with the entire family later in the day. The Coopers were so well off that they employed a cook/housekeeper as well as a chambermaid, and Berenice seemed to have thrived in her new prosperity. She was quite happy to spend hours just sitting around the parlor, talking with her seldom-seen younger son and his guest.

The following day, though, it was down to business. Ferdyn and Adara set out on the horses to a smithy on the south side of town, where he thought it likely they might be able to outfit his lady-love with some armor. "Ferdyn!" the young smith exclaimed as they walked into his forge area through the open door. One of the young adventurer's first acts on arriving "home" had been to make use of a mirror and razor, removing the blond beard that had been growing since before Adara had met him. It made him look younger, and still more handsome. Sigh.

"Greetings, Jean!" Ferdyn said cheerfully. "How's the family?"

"They're all fine," the smith replied. "Bella's expecting another child in the fall. We're hoping for a girl, this time."

"Congratulations, hope you get just what you want," his friend assured him. Pleasantries done with, he moved on to the reason for their visit.

"Adara, this is my friend Jean Smith," Ferdyn said. "Adara is in need of some armor, Jean. I was hoping you might have some of that royal issue stuff that could be fitted for her." Jean cocked an eyebrow, sizing Adara up in her snug-fitting trousers and loose shirt.

"A warrior maiden, huh?" he asked jovially, as he walked off in the direction of a nearby store room.

As the smith went looking to see what might be found, Ferdyn said quietly to Adara, "Jean lost his father in the war, too. He's Rae's age, more or less, but I'm the member of the family that's brought him the most business over the years. He's one of the few smiths in the Carlienne area that works as an armorer. As you can imagine, around here there's a lot more business in tools and farm implements, nails and brackets, barrel hoops and so forth."

Adara smiled up at him. She felt like such a stranger here, among all these people who knew (and liked) Ferdyn. Since they'd begun this journey, she'd frequently had twinges of homesickness. She might have been a bit of an outsider in Pine Hill too, but it was the only home she had really known. Still, until Sarand Bloodspire had been stopped, she could not return to it. Her presence was a risk to everyone there, where the Mancer King knew she had lived.

Five minutes later Jean returned with a double armload of rumpled-looking leather armor. It was clearly used, and old; but it had been maintained with neat's-foot oil over the years and the leather was dark but supple, with no signs of significant deterioration. He held up the hauberk to her shoulders, seeing how it might work.

"I think this set will fit you well enough," the smith said. He worked in leather as well as iron, steel, and other metals. "I'll need to take it in a little though. Come stand over here, and I'll get your measurements." Adara did as she was bid, and in short order Jean had produced a tape measure and was measuring her over her clothes. He did of course have to pull the tape tight around her bust, but she didn't sense any prurient interest from him. After all, he was a married man with a baby on the way.

Soon he was finished. "How soon do you need this?" he asked Adara.

"The sooner the better," she said. "Ferdyn's giving me swordsmanship lessons, and I'm anxious to get armored so I can start practicing with my real weapon." Again a raised eyebrow. After eyeing her speculatively for a moment longer, he returned to the store room for another couple of minutes.

When he returned, he was carrying an outlandish-looking hauberk. It appeared to be a hybrid mail shirt, chainmail hanging from the shoulders and coming down to around mid-thigh, slit to waist level on the sides to allow freedom of movement. But pieces of plate had been riveted to the chain over the areas most in need of protection – the heart, lungs, and belly in front, the kidneys behind.

"This'd be a little big on you," Jean opined. "And it's heavy – but that might work in your favor. If you practice with a heavier weight, you'll feel lighter and more agile when you're actually going into battle." The idea that a slim young woman like Adara would be going into battle, when peace had reigned in the land for most of the young smith's life, didn't seem to faze him. He must have been spending too much time talking with Ferdyn.

"Anyhow," the smith went on, "You're free to borrow this, at no charge, until I can get your regular armor fitted. I have a few projects I need to finish before I can get started, and it'll be three or four days at least until it's ready. I'll need you to come in for a fitting, too, to make sure it all hangs right. You're not exactly the same shape as the man that armor once belonged to."

Adara gave him a brilliant smile. "Thank you, Jean! That will be excellent! Come on Ferdyn, let's go home and get Voleur!" As they walked away from the smithy, lugging the heavy mail shirt with them, Ferdyn wondered at Adara's eagerness. She had shown herself to be a fierce and fearless young woman, but after all of Master Cruztan's cautions he had half expected her to take ship as she'd been advised, ridding herself of the Darkshield once and for all.

They had been socializing with the Cooper family until late, after which Adara had declined his invitation to creep across the hall and join him in his narrow bed last night. And there'd been little enough chance for them to discuss the situation on the ride up here yesterday, with Adara seeming closed off and untalkative.

Now, as they made their way back to the cooperage, Ferdyn broached the subject at last. "Are you sure you want to go through with this, love?" he asked tentatively.

"The Darkshield is a valuable and ancient artifact of great power," Adara tried to explain. "And it's the only thing I have left of my mother. She, and I, are part of a great chain going back two thousand years, Ferdyn! Can't you see how significant that is? It's a chain of love if not of blood, and I would be a coward if I were simply to cast it aside and run away."

"But the two of us, going up against the might of a sorcerer king?" Ferdyn couldn't help asking. He was up for it, he'd go anywhere and do anything for Adara; but he wanted to make sure that she knew what they were getting into. There was a pretty good chance that they might not survive.

"Magus Milegos said that Sarand's fastness is too remote, too mountainous, to be invested with an army," Adara pointed out. "But a small force, one or two people, should be able to creep in undetected. All I need to do is get into his castle and slip some poison into his wine, or a dagger into his neck. It's not like I'm planning a full frontal assault on his entire Swinzen guard, for heaven's sake!"

Ferdyn sighed. She was right, he suspected. But he hated to see his dear girl going into such danger. That he himself would be going into the same danger didn't really worry him much. They rode along, talking of inconsequential things, until they'd reached the family home. Then they walked the horses around to the back.

The cooperage had a spacious outdoor yard behind the main building, and its own large wagon pulled by a team of two cart horses with which they delivered loads of barrels to the wineries, breweries, and distillery in the local area. Those horses were stabled in the carriage house on the far side of the yard, and room had been found within for the visitors' horses as well.

After getting the horses ensconced in stalls, with food and water available, they walked back to the house and prepared for their swordplay session. Ferdyn put on his armor, which he hadn't had on since they'd embarked on their river journey, and fetched Virago from where he'd hung her on a hook in his small bedroom.

Adara collected Voleur, but needed help from Ferdyn to put on the strange mail shirt. It went over the head like a regular shirt, but was considerably less supple than one and heavy as hell. Once she'd gotten it on and had fastened the steel plate collar that added some protection for her throat, she felt as if she were back to carrying her pack. Ugh, fighting in this might be a nightmare, she realized. But she was determined to try. She hoped not to impose on the Coopers' hospitality for any longer than necessary.

Allys had taken the Cooper children with her to visit at a friend's house for the day, but Berenice was at home and she thought it would be fine idea to set up a chair in the large back yard and watch her dashing younger son and his charming young friend practice sword-fighting.

Voleur was a very different thing from the oaken swords they'd been practicing with aboard the *Queen Miranda*. As a bastard-sword, its hilt was long enough for a two-handed grip – yet it was short enough, and light enough, to be wielded with one hand, or would be when Adara had built up her wrist strength.

"Time for some two-handed moves, I think," Ferdyn told her as the two lined up to face each other after they'd limbered up a bit. His Virago was inches longer than Voleur, and his arms were longer as well – a significant advantage of reach. But Adara had agility on her side, even if her opponent had a magically unbreakable blade that lent its wielder stamina and skill.

Adara just watched as Ferdyn showed her the moves, the footwork. What a thing of beauty he was, with that sword in his hands! She felt weighed down by the mail hauberk, but it *was* possible to move in it. Sheathing Virago, Ferdyn said "All right, Adara. Go through that sequence, if you can."

Lunge, retreat, cut, parry. Ferdyn's eyes widened. Adara had been a quick study from the first, picking up what he'd taught her after only seeing it demonstrated a few times and then perfecting her moves with a few hours of practice. Now, with the magus' ring, it appeared she could learn with no time lag at all!

As a test of this theory, before they actually got started sparring, he told her "Better practice sheathing and unsheathing the sword." This was not something he could really teach her, and using a back sheath was one of the trickiest parts of wielding a longsword. To re-sheath your weapon you must train muscle memory to find a narrow slot you could not see.

With a frown of concentration, Adara reached up over her right shoulder and felt around for the opening of the sheath with her fingers. Aha, right there. She fumbled getting Voleur threaded into it, then drew the sword again. The next attempt was smoother, and as Ferdyn watched in astonishment she repeated the maneuver a dozen times – the last four fast and perfect.

A smile of pure delight came over Adara's beautiful face, eyes shining. He realized he had not seen her looking so happy since their meeting with Magus Milegos yesterday morning. He sent a silent prayer of thanks to Baldor for the good fortune that had led the old man to present his lover with that ring. For the first time since they'd learned what they were up against, he had the feeling that they might actually succeed.

"Gee, I wish I'd had this ring a couple of weeks ago!" Adara remarked, the grin still plastered on her face. "Come on, let's spar!" Ferdyn drew Virago, and the two began their graceful, lethal dance. Adara found herself hard-pressed, and it was only the cumbersome hauberk that stood between her and drawn blood on more than one occasion. Her opponent's extra reach, not to mention a decade or so of extra practice, was telling.

They'd been at it for less than an hour, Berenice watching avidly with growing amazement, before Adara was panting for breath and her arms were beginning to feel like lead. Alas, while Voleur was a businesslike blade, it offered her none of the stamina benefits of Virago. And that hauberk was *heavy*.

Lowering her sword almost to the ground, cheeks flushed, Adara said "Whuff! I think that's going to have to be it for the day. Or at least for a couple of hours – I'm exhausted!" Berenice got to her feet with a smile.

"It's time for lunch, anyhow. Come on inside you two, and let's take some refreshment."

Adara soon regained her energy, as they sat eating a vegetable ragout prepared by the Coopers' cook/housekeeper. The exercise had cleared a lot of the negativity from her mind, blowing away the dark clouds that had descended on her after hearing what Magus Milegos had had to say yesterday. They hovered just over the horizon, but for now she was determined to keep them out of her thoughts.

"Mistress Cooper," she asked, "Is there an herbalist shop or apothecary nearby? I'm hoping to craft some potions while I'm here." Berenice looked surprised. The fact that Adara was an herbalist had not yet come up.

"We usually buy our potions and tea herbs from Rena Betony at Greenglade," she said. "There are many such shops in town, of course, but she always has a good selection and it's just a few blocks from here."

"I'll walk you over there after lunch," Ferdyn volunteered. They'd shed their armor and put away their swords, and were dressed in casual clothing once more. Half an hour later they strode along the roadside, Ferdyn's arm around Adara's shoulders.

"That was really amazing today," he remarked. "At the rate that ring accelerates your learning ability, you'll be giving me a stiff contest in no time."

"Mmm, stiff contest..." Adara echoed, with a sly sideways glance. He squeezed her and chuckled. They hadn't made love since night before last, and both of them were beginning to feel a familiar hunger. The sleeping arrangements at the Cooper household were something of a constraint.

As they walked on, Adara said "Yes, the ring is amazing. But I think I'm going to be feeling that practice session pretty soon. Part of what I want to get at the herbalist's is ingredients for liniment." A sympathetic squeeze.

"I'll be happy to rub it in for you," he offered quietly. She gave him a wry grin.

"Thanks, I'm sure I'm going to need it. But I feel kind of... wrong, somehow, to be having sex with you under your mother's roof."

While there was no real theological basis for it, the culture of Tanar tended to frown on extramarital sex. For many, sex inevitably led to babies – and it wasn't good to bring babies into the world without a means of financial support. "We're way up there on the top floor," Ferdyn objected. "If you can keep it down a little, I'm sure nobody will be the wiser." Adara's moans and cries of ecstasy could be a little loud, sometimes.

Glancing around to see that they were unobserved, she reached her left hand down between them and squeezed his right butt cheek. Gods, Ferdyn thought, his pants abruptly getting tighter, I still want her so badly! He'd had many, many lovers since that first one more than a decade ago – and usually once the pursuit was over, the conquest made, his desire had waned. But there was something about Adara that kept him panting for her, even though she'd shared his bed for more than a week.

At Greenglade Adara met Rena, a motherly-seeming woman in her fifties. Ferdyn found himself standing idle or wandering around examining the ingredients, while his lady-love and the herbalist engaged in a long professional discussion. It was more than an hour before they left again.

"Were you able to get everything you needed?" he asked, as they set off toward "home." Ferdyn had been off and living on his own, usually on the road to one adventure or another, for years before the current Cooper residence had been built, so it wasn't really *his* home. He liked the place, though, and was happy to stay there with his family whenever he was in the area.

Adara smiled at him. "I picked up a good supply of the herbs I need for my special tea," she assured him. "And enough ingredients to make quite a few more potions. I gave Rena a sample of my healing salve, and she agreed to buy some from me. I really need to replenish my purse. I don't suppose you happen to know of any untapped ancient tombs in the vicinity?"

Ferdyn grinned back. "Or maybe the odd bandit gang? No, I'm afraid things are awfully settled this close to the capital. After I raided Atylan's tomb and came back with Virago and all that treasure, the word got out and it was picked clean by others before I had the chance to go back. That was the only such place within a short distance of King's Crossing."

Adara sighed. When she'd left Pine Hill she hadn't really considered that she would need money, not only to reach Carlienne but to go after the magus who had killed her parents. She'd studied a map, and this "Bloodspire" fortress was several days' journey on horseback. She'd need warm clothing, too, for though it was now getting on toward the middle of spring the mountains would still be locked in ice and snow.

"It's going to be a couple more days before Jean has my armor ready, I guess," Adara said as they were approaching the cooperage.

"There are some items I want to get that Rena didn't have, things I doubt I'm going to find at any herbalist's shop. Do you think maybe you and I could take a little overnight excursion into the countryside tomorrow?"

Chapter 21

After everyone in the household had gone to bed, a tap came at Ferdyn's door. He'd been fervently hoping to hear just such a tap, and was up like a shot to open the door. Adara stood there wearing a light, nearly transparent nightdress and carrying a freshly-made jar of liniment in one hand.

"Ooh, you're glad to see me," she remarked, casting an admiring glance at the bulge in his drawers. It was a warm night for this time of year, and the drawers were all he had on. Both of them had bathed before dinner, separately. The house had nine bedrooms but only one bathroom.

Ferdyn gathered Adara into his arms. She looked so good by the room's dim lamplight he just wanted to eat her up. There was a problem, though. "Ouch!" she said. "Oh love, my arms and shoulders are *so* sore!"

"All right," he replied, taking the jar of liniment from her. "Off with the nightgown and lie down on your belly, feet toward the pillow." He gestured toward the room's well-padded but narrow bed, a twin to the one in her room across the hall.

He helped her pull off the gown, as lifting her arms up over her head was one of the activities that caused her the most discomfort. She smiled wanly at him, kissed him perfunctorily and then lay down as bidden with a sigh. Ferdyn knelt on a small throw rug at the foot of the bed and opened the jar of liniment. A pungent, herbal odor assailed his nostrils.

"Whoa, what's *in* this stuff?" he asked. While she'd been working in the kitchen he'd spent most of the rest of the afternoon over at the cooperage, hanging out with Raedyn and the crew. Adara, whose head was turned to one side so she could breath, smiled at him. "A little of this, a little of that," was all she would say. "It's another of Nanny Selden's patented recipes, I'm afraid." She really *was* serious about not revealing those trade secrets, Ferdyn realized.

The jar's fragrant contents were an off-white color and the consistency of a heavy cream, but when he scooped some out with his fingertips it immediately began to melt and flow, easily gliding over the skin of Adara's back, shoulders, neck and arms. He pulled her long, silken black hair out of the way with his left hand and began rubbing the liniment in, using his strong fingers to knead the sore muscles.

Adara relaxed, sagging as if all of the air had been let out of her, and moaned in ecstasy. "Ooooh, that's so good!" she murmured, and Ferdyn found his cock growing rigid. It had been days, and between the sight of Adara naked on his bed and those moans so reminiscent of the sounds she made during sex, he was having a very hard time concentrating on the task at hand.

When liniment had been spread all over the sore areas Ferdyn capped the jar and set it on the nightstand. Then he climbed on top of Adara, perched on her firm buttocks and taking some of his weight on his knees as he used both hands to massage the liniment in. For a while his hands and fingertips were tingling, and the skin of Adara's upper body was glowing pink. Then it seemed as if the liniment had been completely absorbed, and the smell became just a faint hint. "Don't stop rubbing me, it feels so wonderful," Adara pleaded.

"Just a second," Ferdyn said. He hastily climbed down and kicked off his drawers. Then, cock jutting, he resumed his perch. He worked his way down her spine, popping her vertebrae, and kneading the knotted muscles until they were as soft as butter. More moans. His erection was nestled between Adara's buttocks like a sausage in a roll, warm and throbbing.

Though Adara had been focused on the wonderful sensations of the back rub, that hot presence at her rear had not gone unnoticed. The liniment and Ferdyn's ministrations had done their work, and she now had almost none of the aching and stiffness that had been growing since this morning's unaccustomed workout.

Keeping her head down, resting it on her arms, she wriggled a little. Ferdyn got the idea and went up on his knees so that Adara could get her own knees beneath her. She scooted up until she had her butt up, with him kneeling behind her. Yes!

Ferdyn stuck two fingers of his right hand in his mouth, noticing that there was no residue of the medicinal liniment left. Then he put those fingers down between Adara's buttocks, and found her vulva swollen and glistening. It appeared she was ready and eager for this new position, and he was more than happy to oblige her.

Backing off just a little, he guided his stiff cock to the opening and pushed slowly inside. Adara moaned softly, backing into him slightly as he went all the way in. "Oh baby, you feel so good to me," he murmured softly, then added "Let's try to remember to keep the noise down..."

The other half of Adara's pre-Ferdyn sex education had involved spending time on farms around Pine Hill in the springtime, observing bulls mounting cows and stallions mounting mares. The sight of their enormous rampant cocks had both fascinated and repelled her. But being in the mare's position now triggered a mental image that sent a surge of animal lust through her. It had her tripping on the edge of orgasm almost as soon as her "stallion" had entered her.

Stifling a scream, Adara bucked and vibrated as Ferdyn plunged into her, over and over again – harder, and faster, and oh! They collapsed to the surface of the bed moments later, panting and grinning. "Adara!" Ferdyn murmured close her ear. "What did you *do* to me?" He slipped out, and she rolled over so they could embrace face to face. "We'll take it slower next time," she said quietly.

Chapter 22

Thank the gods, the weather was clear and warm as Adara and Ferdyn, mounted on Zarhya and Simdal, trotted out along the road leading east from King's Crossing. Along this highway, he'd promised her, were many farms, vineyards, and country estates – interspersed with woodlands where she should be able to find every kind of herbal ingredient from leaves and flowers to fungi and roots. The middle of spring was the ideal season for such harvesting.

The dark clouds still hovered below Adara's horizon, but the beauty of the spring morning (and the satisfaction of their lovemaking last night) was doing a wonderful job of keeping them at bay. She glanced up to her left, north to the snow-covered peaks that were just visible through the morning mist.

The Neigande mountains, even here at their taller western end, were considerably lower than the Crestan range far to the east. But they'd do if you were looking for something steep, cold, and inhospitable. And soon, all too soon, she would be going there.

Adara had not brought either Voleur or the borrowed hauberk with her, relying on her bow, her dagger, and her special relationship with the elementals – not to mention the magnificent young man at her side – to protect her if the need arose. They planned to be out only overnight and return to King's Crossing tomorrow, so she had plenty of room in her pack for the ingredients she hoped to collect.

The road began to bend toward the northeast ahead, skirting a range of low hills covered in oak woodland. Adara nudged Zarhya into a canter, riding easily, and marveling at the joy of being atop a horse that actually had speeds faster than "quick walk." She cast a thought back to poor old Bulo, hoping he was being treated kindly by his new owners on their farm outside of Grandwyl.

Ferdyn brought Simdal up beside her, grinning in appreciation of her new riding skills, and the two left the road at the bend and went up into the hills. Several meadows and a few rotten logs later, Adara had quite a collection of botanicals resting in her pack. She'd brought a double handful of little muslin drawstring bags, to keep the specimens separated.

They picnicked in the woods, then picked up the road again on the north side of the hills and continued on their way. There was still one ingredient Adara was hoping to find, and she was surprised that she had not yet encountered it. It was a fairly common plant, ornamental enough to be included in many gardens. But what gardens existed in Carlienne and King's Crossing were mostly private, hidden away.

Grapevines grew on either side of the road here, and off some distance to the north they saw a manor house, a chateau in the new style, sitting on a slight rise. Adara pulled up and shaded her eyes with a hand, peering at it. "Is that smoke, Ferdyn?" she asked. "Probably," he said. "Those places have dozens of fireplaces…" "But it's a warm spring afternoon," she objected. "Why would they have a roaring, smoky fire going?"

After a moment's study Ferdyn had to agree with her. "There's the drive," he said, pointing to a break in the vineyards up ahead. "Let's go see!" Delighted to be given their heads, the two young Khoureshis pelted along the narrow, hard-packed dirt road at a full gallop. The manor house was only a mile away, and in a couple of minutes Adara and Ferdyn were racing past a gatehouse and along a semicircular drive that fronted the grand building.

It had tall columns all along the front, with spacious lawns and a large reflecting pool just past the drive. And from two of the top-storey windows, flames and smoke were pouring. The front doors were standing open, and a squadron of servants had formed a bucket brigade from the pond to the front door – and presumably, up the stairs to where the fire was burning.

A well-dressed couple Adara took to be the owners of the house were standing ashen faced, wringing their hands and watching as the flames overpowered the efforts to douse them. Clearly, the fire had gotten too much of a head start on them. A bucketful of water every few seconds wasn't going to be enough to stop the whole place from going up.

She hopped down from her horse and ran to stand near the pond, not far from where a man who looked like a butler was scooping up another bucketful of water. The next empty bucket was still six hands away. In a moment she had called on Onden, and twin columns of water rose from the pool and flew thirty feet through the air to pour in through the windows where the flames were to be seen. There was a hissing sound, and steam became mixed with the billowing smoke.

Again, Adara silently begged the water elemental. And again, her request was granted. All four of the elementals tended to be a little like capricious children on occasion, and you could not always count on them to do what you wanted. In the case of Salomand, he often did far *more* than you wanted. But Onden was the sweetest among them, and Adara had inherited a warm and friendly relationship with her thanks to being Nanny Selden's protégé. A third gout of water, the level of the water in the pool now halfway down to the bottom, and the servants reported that the fire was out.

All now gathered around Adara, foremost among them the householder and his wife. They were looking at her in awe. The man, an aristocratic-looking fellow in his sixties, bowed low. "Thank you, madam magus, for your timely intervention!" he cried. She thought she probably looked like no magus the world had ever seen; but she didn't want to go into lengthy explanations, or use the word "witch," so she made no attempt to correct him.

Adara supposed a curtsy was appropriate, but since she was dressed in her traveling leathers she settled for a deep bow. "Glad to be of service, sir," she said. "It was fortunate that my companion and I happened by at just this moment. As you can see from our garb, we have been out gathering ingredients for magic potions." She wasn't sure there *was* such a thing as magic potions, though some people might think the ones she crafted with mundane ingredients were magical in effect. Whatever the case, the gentleman seemed happy to accept whatever their savior had to say.

"I am Viscount Luis de Grenvale," he went on, "and this is my wife Madeleine. Please, come inside and partake of our hospitality." Adara and Ferdyn introduced themselves, and were ushered into the de Grenvales' front parlor. Half the staff seemed to have been mobilized to ensure that the fire was completely out and begin dealing with the damage, while the other half had returned to their usual duties.

The Viscount's gratitude knew no bounds. They were given tea and cakes, then bade to stay the night. With the fire completely out and the windows in the house left open for several hours, the smell of smoke had almost completely dissipated by suppertime.

Luckily the viscountess was of a similar tall and slender build, and she was able to loan their young benefactress a dress for the formal meal. When Adara had planned this trip, sitting down to dinner with the nobility had been the last thing on her mind. By now the household had swollen to a further nine family members – the de Grenvales' son and daughter and their spouses and children. The eldest grandson was Adara's age, and kept staring at her across the dinner table in a way that made her uneasy and left Ferdyn simmering.

But even Ferdyn, usually so brash and well-spoken, seemed a little ill-at-ease in this exalted company. His family were prosperous tradesmen, solidly established in the upper middle class; but that did not make them social equals with the gentry. As for Adara, she had decided to let her mystique as "madam magus" carry her along, and did quite well. They spent the night sleeping in lavish (separate) bedrooms on the second floor, and breakfasted with the family in the morning.

Back in her traveling leathers once again, Adara was gazing out the glassed-in windows of the breakfast room to the gardens beyond. Maridem, she thought, as she washed down a slice of warm quiche with a mouthful of sweetened tea, you are surely looking after me. For there, amid the other shrubbery in the five acres of manicured grounds surrounding the chateau, was the very plant she'd been looking for and had not yet found: beautiful, deadly Nerium.

As they were taking their leave of their hosts, and thanking them for their delightful hospitality, Viscount de Grenvale pressed a leather purse into her hand. "A token of our immense gratitude," he said. "Without you, we would likely have spent the night sleeping in the barn – assuming the fire had not spread to it. You have saved our ancestral home."

"You are too generous, viscount," Adara said graciously, "and I thank you in return. And might I beg one further boon from you?"

"Certainly, anything!" the old man replied. Adara wondered if he would have been so nice if she'd been a wall-eyed crone instead of an attractive young woman, but let the thought pass.

"I see you have some lovely vegetation in your gardens. Would you mind if I took a few clippings?"

Chapter 23

"Hold still," Louis commanded. Adara stood with her legs apart and her arms outstretched, as he made some marks on the dark-stained, supple leather with a piece of chalk he held in his hand. Ferdyn stood by, looking on with amusement. Louis' initial alteration of the old suit of armor, which had once protected some nameless soldier of the Elvany War, had been a good one. But the smith took pride in his work, and wanted to make sure that Adara's armor fit her perfectly. She would need to be wearing it, possibly day and night, for some time to come.

His own armor, handed down from his dead father, had not needed any alteration. True, it had hung on him a bit when he had first put it on at age nineteen, but he had filled out over the years and was apparently now the image of the late Samdyn Cooper. Or at least, the same size and shape as that unfortunate man had been when he'd been killed in a freak mishap at the age of thirty-four.

A few more adjustments were made to the fit of the hauberk, as Adara stood there wearing the greaves and her linen shirt; then she put it on once again. "All right, pretend you're swinging your sword!" Louis told her, and she went into a swordsman's stance. They'd had two more practice sessions using the borrowed mail shirt, and she had not even needed liniment after the second one. Now, she seemed to have all the moves down completely. Ferdyn knew only too well, though, that sword training was not at all the same thing as battle. On the other hand, he had seen Adara kill before and she had acquitted herself well enough. She would be fine, he told himself.

The fit was declared to be perfect, and Adara handed over the two marks that had been agreed on as a price. Viscount de Grenvale's reward for saving his ancestral manor house had proven to be fifty gold marks – a small fortune – and Adara had been jubilant. She was sure it was an indication that Mother Maridem was on her side in her fight against the Mancer King.

She opted to keep the armor on for the ride back to the cooperage, even strapping on her back sheath and Voleur. What a pair they made, in their matching armor – each with a mighty sword at their backs. Ferdyn had a vision of the demon bringer's minions turning tail and fleeing at the very sight of them. Adara's thoughts were elsewhere.

That was the last item on the checklist, she thought. Well, she needed to lay in some grain for Zarhya and gather up her pack. But she felt that she was now pretty much ready to go. She'd made up a lot more of her favorite potions, including more of the liniment and healing salve. And her kit now included four little bottles of the deadly Nerium extract. She'd dipped several of her arrows in it and carefully dried the tips, marking the shafts below the fletchings with a little red thread. If she could just get within arrow shot of an enemy, they would be dead in a minute or two even if only shot in an arm or leg.

They had another jolly dinner with the Cooper family that evening. The tale of their overnight stay at Chateau de Grenvale had been a huge hit, and was still making the rounds of Berenice and Allys' friends and acquaintances. They might not entirely approve of Ferdyn and his unconventional lifestyle, but they loved him in spite of it – and it did make for great conversation.

Once again, Adara slipped into Ferdyn's room after everyone had gone to bed. They made love slowly, passionately, clinging together as if they would never let go. But as they lay in the afterglow, Adara did not seem as utterly relaxed and at peace as usual. If anything, she seemed a little on edge. "Worried about Sarand Bloodspire?" he murmured, squeezing her to him. Spent, he was having a hard time remaining conscious.

Adara hugged him tightly. "A bit," she admitted softly. Ferdyn stroked her hair and kissed her on the forehead.

"Don't you worry about a thing, baby," he assured her drowsily. "Tomorrow we'll talk it out and figure out exactly how we'll take him down. You and I, we're unstoppable."

She nodded sleepily, kissed him, and went back to her own room. It wouldn't have been possible for the two of them to get a good night's sleep sharing the narrow beds probably intended for the as-yet-unborn Cooper heirs. Blissfully satisfied, Ferdyn dropped off into a delicious sleep.

He woke to morning sunshine coming in through the bedroom window, sparkling on the myriad little panes that made up the glass. Glass windows like these were just one of the many touches that made this house a standout in King's Crossing. Smiling to himself as he remembered making love with Adara the night before, Ferdyn yawned and stretched. Then he relieved himself in the chamberpot before getting into his clothes. Casual trousers, a cloth shirt, and boots should be good enough for today. He supposed they would have to end their lazy sojourn and get back on the road tomorrow.

Stepping across the hall, Ferdyn rapped on Adara's door. "Rise and shine, sleepyhead," he said fondly. It was unusual for her not to be up with the dawn. Hearing nothing he rapped again, and then tried the handle. The door swung open on an empty room.

The bed was neatly made, and there was no sign of Adara's pack or other belongings. Atop the bed was a folded piece of parchment, with his name printed on it in large letters: FERDYN. His heart caught in his throat as he snatched it off the coverlet and opened it up. It read:

Dear Ferdyn,

Good news! You will not have to go and beard the Mancer King in his den. I have changed my mind, and decided to go back to Rivermarch. With my new battle skills I should be able to kill off any more Swinzen old Sarand cares to send my way, until he gets tired of trying. Then I can go back to my pleasant, quiet life as a village herbalist, marry some nice local boy and settle down. It's been lots of fun meeting you, and I'll always remember our time together. Thanks for all you've done to help me. Go raid some more tombs, and stay away from the demon bringer.

Best wishes and fond regards,

Adara

Ferdyn's face was a mask of shock and anger as he hurled the note to the surface of the bed. The idiot girl! His heart ached as he rushed back to his room and began climbing into his armor. Then he strapped Virago to his back, and stuffed the rest of his belongings into his pack before pounding down the stairs.

Berenice, Allys, and the children looked up in him in surprise as Ferdyn came hurtling into the dining room lugging his pack. His eyes were wide, his face grim. "Mother, can I beg some supplies from the kitchen?"

"What is it?" she started to ask, but seeing his expression she jumped up from where she'd been sipping her tea and went with him into the kitchen.

"Mary," Berenice directed the cook, who was just taking a tray of pastries out of the oven, "Please give Ferdyn whatever he needs." And money, he thought, desperately trying to remember everything he needed before running off. He'd expected to have a whole day in which to plan.

"And can I borrow five marks, Mother?" he asked, calming down a little.

While he was stuffing food and drink into his pack, she went to the parlor and returned with a handful of coins. "You needn't pay it back, dear," she said sweetly. "Without your contributions, the family would never have gotten to where it is today."

"Thank you Mama," Ferdyn said, hugging her gently and giving her a kiss on the cheek. He made to go out the back door, in the direction of the cooperage carriage house. "I've got to go now," he said in parting. "I have to catch her!"

Chapter 24

Dawn was breaking over the hills to the east, bathing the road in pink light, and Adara swayed in the saddle. Zarhya had begun at a walk as they crept carefully away from the cooperage; but once they had left King's Crossing behind she had been going at a canter for a few miles, then a trot, then a canter again. Now she was walking so slowly Bulo could have overtaken her – head down, as tired as her rider.

It was no use, Adara realized. She had to stop and rest. She *hoped* that Ferdyn would read her letter and search for her, if he sought her at all, on the road east to Rivermarch. But she had the feeling she had blundered there. If she had truly wanted to convince him that she cared nothing for him, and that she planned to return home and face any of Sarand's demons that came with her sword, she should have picked a fight with him and let him *see* her riding off south toward Carlienne and the river road.

Her tears had long since dried. I'm a coward, she thought mournfully. Somehow it had seemed so much easier to just slip away in the night, leaving a note behind. She doubted her ability to successfully lie to Ferdyn in person – he would have seen into her heart in a moment, and she could never have brought herself to be cruel to him.

Away to the east Adara spotted a line of trees that undoubtedly meant there was a stream. A place to water poor Zarhya and let her have a bag of oats. Adara had taken them from the fodder stores at the cooperage, and left coins behind to pay for what she'd taken.

Moving in among the trees to the waterside, Adara let the horse drink. Then she removed the bridle, replacing it with a halter, and tied on a feedbag full of oats. "Sorry old girl, the saddle's got to stay," she told the patient animal. She removed the pack from where it was tied behind the saddle though, and spread her bedroll under the tree. They were more or less invisible from the road, she hoped.

After squatting to relieve herself and having a few bites to eat and a pull from a water skin, Adara lay down on the bedroll and dropped off into a troubled sleep. The new armor was, surprisingly, comfortable enough to sleep in. At least, it was if it had been more than twenty-four hours since you'd last slept.

Zarhya whickered and Adara's eyes popped open. How long had she been sleeping? The sun was now high in the sky but hadn't yet reached its zenith, so probably four or five hours had elapsed. Not a full night's sleep, but enough for her to go on a while longer.

The mare had long since finished the oats, and was annoyed to find the feed bag prohibited her from cropping the lush grass that grew in among the trees. Adara got the bag off and let the poor neglected creature eat a little, as she set about getting herself ready to go. The pack went back up behind the saddle, the bridle replaced the halter, and the rider mounted again. Onward, but this time at a gentler pace.

The horse had recovered enough of her strength that she was able to move along at a steady, ground-eating trot until the sun was well down toward the western horizon, with only a couple of short breaks in between. To Adara's relief there had been almost no traffic on the road today. This far north there was mostly only local commerce, and in the middle of spring relatively few farmers had crops to take to market.

They came to Dunstadt, a medium-sized market village, and Adara took a room for the night at the inn. She made sure that the horse would be stabled indoors, not visible to any casual passersby. A hot meal by the fireside, a glass of wine to help her sleep the more soundly, and she was tucking herself into bed (and crossing her fingers that there were no bedbugs) by shortly past sunset. As she lay there, trying to drift off to sleep, a wave of sadness came over her. Oh Ferdyn, what else could I do? There were tears on her cheeks as she sank into slumber.

The next morning Adara woke feeling restored. Leaving Ferdyn had been hard, but doing so assured he would be safe – and that the Mancer King would possess no power to coerce her into handing over the Darkshield. Her optimism rising, she and Zarhya hit the road right after breakfast and moved along at a comfortable pace.

The further north the road took them, the less there was to see on it. They rode through a broad valley given over to pastureland, with sheep and cattle grazing on either side. Finally toward evening a tiny village appeared. There were three or four dwellings clustered near the road, and a small inn with a sign out front reading "The Sandman."

The Sandman offered no stables, but there was a fenced yard behind the building where Zarhya could be hitched for the night while partaking of hay, grain, and water. It would have to do. An idea had been growing in Adara's mind as the miles had rolled away today, with no company but her thoughts. Beyond a doubt, the magus' ring worked as advertised. She had very nearly become an expert swordsman after a few days of practice with Voleur, and she now rode as if she'd been in the saddle for years. But for the next skill she wished to perfect she would need shelter.

After leaving Zarhya with a boy around back, Adara hefted her pack and walked around to the front door of the Sandman. The small common room was dimly lit, and all transactions were apparently handled by the woman on duty at the bar. She was past forty and looked as if she'd had a hard life, but seemed kindly enough.

"Welcome to Sand Creek," she said, pausing from a probably unnecessary mopping of the bar with a damp rag. There were no other customers in the place.

"Thank you," Adara said shortly. "I'm in need of a private room for the night. Do you have one?" That elicited a smile, revealing teeth that were brown but strong-looking. Setting down her rag, the proprietress came around from behind the bar.

"Just for the one night, then?" she asked, leading the way down a dimly lit hallway.

Adara smiled to herself as she considered what circumstances might lead one to put up in a place like Sand Creek for longer than a single night. Perhaps if she were a livestock buyer? There didn't seem to be anything else in the region worth coming here for, save that it was along the road she must travel.

Adara was shown into a room, and handed over a couple of shillings for the night's lodging. Private it was, and there was a lock on the door. But it was the size of a large closet. She nearly had to walk sideways to squeeze past the bed, so that she could set her pack down on the floor and not block the aisle. The narrow bed was the room's only furnishing.

Shrugging, Adara removed her armor. It was comfortable enough to have on for hours at a time, and not at all bad for riding. Plus it gave her a feeling of security – should she be ambushed by bandits, there was a chance their arrows would be deflected. Beneath the armor she was wearing her leather trousers and a linen shirt, and she put on her leather jerkin over the top of the shirt for warmth. The altitude was beginning to climb, and nights were cold this early in the season.

Soon Adara was joined by other customers in the inn's small common room. Two sat at the bar, chatting familiarly with the proprietress, while the other eyed her speculatively but did not intrude when she gave him no encouragement. All of them dined on coarse bread with fresh-churned butter and bowls of mutton stew.

Not long after eating Adara returned to her room, latched and barred the door, and lay down on the bed fully dressed. She closed her eyes, and began reaching out with her mind. This technique, which Nanny Selden called "riding," had been one the "tricks and powers" in which Adara had been trained as an apprentice. But while she'd been able to cozen favors from the elementals from the age of twelve, riding was considerably more difficult – and more hazardous. She had only actually done it once before, with Nanny standing by to assist her – and call her back, if needed.

Outside it was dark, and that darkness was lit here and there by sparks big and small. These were living creatures, their life force appearing in Adara's visualization like glowing candles. Some, the lives of creatures like insects, were so tiny they barely glittered in her mental vision. Others were larger – a candle, a lantern, a bonfire. Sentient creatures, her fellow humans, glowed brightest of all; but those she could not ride.

For long minutes Adara just lay motionless on the bed, as if asleep or in a deep trance, while she extended her awareness out around the environs of Sand Creek. She identified each spark she saw – the blazes that were the proprietress and her customers, the human occupants of the houses, dogs and cats, mice and rats. As she practiced this she felt her range increase. The ring, as she'd hoped and expected, worked as well for this skill as it had for the others!

Finally Adara felt ready to slip inside one of the creatures she'd pinpointed. One could ride passively, sliding in unnoticed alongside the animal's mind and simply receiving the input of its senses as it went about its own business. Or, one could override that mind – pushing it into the background and taking full control.

That latter technique was the most perilous for the rider, Nanny had warned. Becoming an animal, using its abilities to do what one wished, could lead one to become so absorbed in that form that one's own form was left behind, forgotten, to die.

In a fallow field a quarter of a mile west of the inn a mouse stirred, searching among the spring shoots for insects. Adara's consciousness slipped into its body, and was disoriented as she suddenly found herself looking at a world gone murky. The nocturnal creature's night vision was far superior to her own, but its eyes did not provide the range of detail she was used to. A great deal of its information was coming from its ears, nose, and delicate little paws, and she lacked the experience to interpret that information.

The little rodent's fan-like ears detected the faint ticking of a scuttling beetle, and in a split second it had pounced. It sat on its haunches, eagerly devouring the crunchy morsel. Oh, gross! Adara thought. She removed her awareness and sought another target.

The proprietress of the Sandman kept a cat on the premises, and Adara was soon listening to the conversation in the common room through the creature's ears. The furball had been curled up asleep beside the hearth, and Adara passively listened through its much more acute sense of hearing as the locals discussed feed prices, wolves, and the coming shearing.

Scarcely worth listening in on, but as a proof of the ability it was stunning! Who would dream that a dumb animal asleep in a corner was actually a human eavesdropper? Excited, feeling her powers grow, Adara reached out and entered the body of a lamb dozing in a sheepfold at a ranch a mile away. She opened its eyes and moved around, then took a few tentative steps.

Oop! Making four legs produce a coordinated walk was harder than she'd expected. The creature stumbled, waking it up, and then fought for a moment in blind panic when it realized someone else was controlling its movements. Not wishing to create an uproar that would bring the shepherd, Adara backed off her control while remaining inside. Could she exert a *partial* control, letting the animal handle navigation while she dictated where it would go?

That was, after all, pretty much how ordinary riding was done. Zarhya had control of her own legs, but Adara directed her using the reins. Exerting enough control to prevent the lamb from baa-ing in fright and trying to sooth its mind through the power of her will, she got the little creature settled down. Let's go over to the water trough now, she suggested forcefully. And the lamb went.

Later than she would ordinarily have gone to sleep, Adara drew herself back to her body and undressed for bed. She soon drifted off, satisfied that she had added a new, devastating weapon to her arsenal. Watch out, Mancer King!

Chapter 25

Three days later, Adara was convinced that she had gotten away from Ferdyn cleanly. All those hours on the road, and she had seen no fellow travelers. A few farmers and other locals were moving on the north road as it rose into the foothills of the Neigandes, but sometimes she would see no one at all for hours at a time. She'd taken to carrying on long conversations with Zarhya, who had proven to be an excellent listener.

This town, Baadzen, was the last on the north road officially a part of the kingdom of Tanar. Beyond it was only Kragstein and its Bloodspire – the terminus of the road and the entirety of the "kingdom" ruled over by the Mancer King. Baadzen stood at an elevation of around three thousand feet and was something of a destination for travelers – though usually not until the summer months. It offered mineral hot springs that were supposed to provide health benefits for all who bathed in their waters.

Adara didn't know about the health benefits, though certainly the application of heat could bring relief from afflictions of the joints. And her butt, after days in the saddle, could definitely use some relief. The main bathhouse in town was not yet open for the season, as there was still snow on the ground. But the Maridem's Waters inn, over near the west side of town, had its own sex-segregated bathhouse where patrons could soak in pools full of hot water piped in from the nearby springs.

She still had plenty of money left from the viscount's boon, and Adara decided to treat herself to a little luxury. After all, she'd been dressed in armor and riding hard every day, practicing her mind-riding and studying the maps and other materials she'd brought with her before falling into an exhausted sleep each night. And tomorrow, perhaps, she would die.

Tonight she would have a wonderful hot bath, change into some decent clothes, have a nice meal in the common room, and pump the locals for information about the situation in Kragstein. Was it true the entire populace of that small city was enthralled?

The management provided long, voluminous robes, thick towels, and even soft cloth slippers for the customers to wear to and from the bathhouses out back. Thus clad, Adara entered the women's side and found a room built all of stone with two good-sized pools set into the floor. Several older women were relaxing in them, and steam filled the air. A smile, the first such expression to appear on her face in days, came unbidden as she hung up her robe on one of the hooks provided and walked down the steps into the hip-deep hot pool.

Oh, that was marvelous! Mother Maridem take me now, Adara thought dreamily, as she lay back and let the warmth claim her. It was almost, if not quite, worth the five-day trip on horseback to get here. Her anxieties washed away for the moment, she floated in the water and let her mind drift to other things. Hadn't the ancients built baths like these heated, not by natural hot springs, but by chambers beneath stoked with burning wood? They ought to build one of those in Carlienne!

When all of her aches had been soaked away and her fingers and toes were getting too wrinkly to tolerate, Adara reluctantly climbed back out of the hot pool and dried herself off with the towel before putting on her robe and slippers again. A young girl attendant stood by to collect wet towels, putting them into a bin whence they'd be laundered for re-use.

Adara padded back through the corridor connecting the bathhouse with the main part of the inn, oblivious to any looks she might be getting from other inn patrons. She was horny, definitely. She had left her lover behind, and didn't know if she'd ever have another one. She *hoped* she would. Maybe once Sarand Bloodspire was destroyed she could get Ferdyn back. Nah, he would probably never forgive her for deceiving him.

Reaching into the pocket of her robe, Adara fumbled for the key to her room. She turned it in the lock and opened the door. It was nearly dark out now, and in any case the room's window was shuttered and latched. She'd left an oil lamp burning on the bedside table, but the light it cast was dim. After coming in from the brightly lit corridor, it took a moment for her eyes to adjust.

When they did, Adara stifled a scream. There was a man, clad in the same sort of robe she was wearing, lying on her bed. "Hello, Adara," he said softly, not smiling. Ferdyn!

Damn, damn, damn! Now it was not a scream Adara had to stifle, but the urge to run over there and fall into his arms. He had clearly recently been in the men's bathhouse himself, and he looked good enough to eat. His face sported a few days' growth of beard, as it had the moment she had first laid eyes on him. Was that truly less than a month ago?

Ferdyn sat up on the bed and put his feet on the floor, gazing at Adara hungrily. If he'd hoped for a warm reception, he was out of luck. "Damn you! What are you *doing* here?" she demanded furiously. His face fell, warm brown eyes taking on a hurt puppy-dog look. How the hell did a grown man the size of Ferdyn manage that?

He shrugged and got to his feet, the robe falling open. His cock was on the rise, and Adara bit her lip. "I came for *you* of course, dear girl," he said. "Did you imagine for one moment that I believed that crock of shit about your returning to Rivermarch? 'Best wishes and fond regards'? Did you think I would just roll over and say 'oh well,' and go find myself another lover? Perhaps while I was out 'raiding some tombs'?"

Adara stared at him in consternation, arms straight down at her sides. She hung her head, lip quivering, and tears began rolling down her cheeks. In an instant Ferdyn had closed the distance between them and enfolded her in his arms, kissing the top of her head. "Adara, I *love* you, I truly do," he said softly. "I can't let you go into deadly danger alone."

"B-but it's *because* I love you that I can't let you c-come along!" Adara wailed, burying her face in his shoulder and shaking with sobs as he held her tight.

"There, there…" Ferdyn said, patting her on the back and continuing to plant little kisses on her head. His erection was subsiding.

He put an arm around Adara and led her back to the bed, urging her to sit down. Then, with a regretful glance down at his now-flaccid member, he tied his robe closed again. "If only you hadn't run off like that, love," he said softly, his arm around her as her crying began to trail off. "We're smart people, and I'm sure we can think of a way to do this so Sarand can't use me as a pawn to coerce you. Have you eaten yet?" Adara shook her head miserably, looking around for a handkerchief. She'd been so relaxed and happy just a few minutes ago, and now her damned nose was running!

Ferdyn rose from the bed, and picked up the bundle of clothing he'd dropped on the dresser on the far side of it. "Come on dear, let's put on some clothes and have something to eat and drink. I know you'll feel better, and then we can talk this out. If we really can't figure out a plan, I'll just wait for you here while you go storm the castle. All right?"

Nodding miserably, Adara dug a handkerchief out of her pack and dabbed her eyes and nose. Then she began putting on the outfit she'd been planning to wear earlier – before her clever plan had collapsed so utterly. When they were both dressed, she stepped up to Ferdyn and threw her arms around him, giving him a long, hard kiss. "I've missed you," she admitted before releasing him. They went down the stairs and took a seat near the fire.

This was not your run-of-the mill "choice of whatever's in the pot over the fire" sort of inn. There was an actual menu with five items on it, written in chalk on a board beside the bar. They both ordered the roast beef, which came with roasted potatoes and gravy, hearty slices of fresh bread with butter, and new spring peas. The residents of Baadzen liked their food to pack a caloric punch, up here in the mountains.

By the time Adara and Ferdyn had finished the meal, along with the bottle of excellent red wine they'd ordered to accompany it, she especially was feeling a *lot* better. They held hands across the table for a while, just drinking in the sight of each other's faces.

Both of them were thinking, though. "I had planned," Adara said at last, "to spend some time in the common room tonight listening to local gossip. I thought I might learn what to expect in Kragstein. Surely you-know-who couldn't really have the entire town locked down and under his control?" Ferdyn grinned at her, that cheerful smile that had warmed her heart since she'd first seen it.

"Excellent idea," he said. "Maybe we should go sit at the bar?"

They relocated from their cozy table and squeezed into the space at the center of the bar. Locals and regulars were much likelier to do their drinking there. "What can I get you?" the grizzled bartender asked.

Ferdyn looked to Adara, who said "That wine was pretty good. Shall we get another bottle?" Her companion raised an eyebrow, but nodded to the bartender and shortly they were sipping more glasses of the delicious red. The western part of Tanar, it was said, had the finest vintages in the world.

As the bartender was uncorking the bottle, Ferdyn remarked "The baths here are very enjoyable. But we were disappointed to find the main baths in town closed. Do you know when they open?" The man poured a little of the wine into each of their glasses. This was a high-class establishment.

"It depends on the weather, mostly," he replied. "Usually late Flora, early Quicken. Whenever the snows melt."

Ferdyn nodded thanks to the bartender, and then raised his glass to Adara. "Here's to us, love," he said. "But next anniversary, let's go someplace warmer." The bartender eyed them dubiously.

"It's your anniversary?" he asked. Adara might possibly be mistaken for older than seventeen, but not by a lot.

"Yes, our second!" Ferdyn replied with a smile. "We came all the way up here from Dunstadt hoping to see the famous hot springs, but we hadn't realized they're not a year-round thing. So now we're here, and it's a long ride home. What about this Kragstein place, up at the end of the road? Is that worth a look? Pretty mountain scenery, maybe?"

You're kind of laying it on with a trowel dear, Adara thought, but she just kept a blank smile on her face and gazed at Ferdyn as if he were the only thing worth looking at in her universe. Truth to tell, she'd much sooner look at him than anybody else in this establishment. Though the young fellow down at the far end of the bar was kind of cute...

The bartender's neutral expression turned to a scowl. "Better you just enjoy the baths here for a few days and then go home," he warned. "You don't want to be going up to Kragstein." Time for her to contribute, Adara thought.

She put on an expression of bright interest and said, "Ooh! What is it? Werewolves? Vampires?" Folklore frequently populated the regions near isolated mountain castles with such creatures.

The bartender gave a wry grin. "Werewolves and vampires would probably be an improvement," he said. "I'm surprised you hadn't heard about it, coming from Dunstadt. Kragstein's ruled by the Mancer King, him as lives up in the Bloodspire. He's a powerful magus, and a bad 'un. Has all these pig-men demons running things for him."

Adara eyed him skeptically. "Demons? Seriously?" The barman put both hands on the bar and looked her seriously in the eyes.

"They're real, missus. As real as you and me, and I've talked to plenty who've seen them. Kragstein's so high up in the mountains they have to bring in most of their food from lower down, so there's people coming through here all the time with carts of produce. They say you'll be let in through the gates if you've got food to sell, but otherwise you can forget about it. And a pretty girl like you, they might not let you leave."

Ferdyn took a turn. "But why go so far out of your way to sell a load of turnips? Surely it would make more sense to stay away from there, if there's demons like you say." A grim smile.

"Gold," the barman said. "Red gold, from beneath the Bloodspire. They'll pay double, triple, what you'd get anyplace else for turnips, potatoes, cabbages, and grain."

Adara looked at him wide-eyed. "What did you mean," she asked tremulously, "when you said they 'might not let me leave'?"

"It's just what they say," the barman admitted. "I haven't actually talked with anyone who had a girl snatched. But it's said the Mancer King has a taste for young, pretty girls. Any he wants, he just casts his spell and she'll be his love-slave for as long as he wants. When he tires of them, he turns them over to his demon guards for their sport." She did not have to feign a shudder.

Ferdyn picked up his wine glass and got to his feet. Half the bottle remained, and he took that as well. "Very interesting," he said. "I suppose we'll head back toward Dunstadt, then." Turning to Adara he added with a leer, "What do you say we take this back to our room, dear?" She picked up her own glass, and the two of them went back up the stairs.

Chapter 26

They set the bottle and glasses on the room's small table, then seated themselves. Adara eyed Ferdyn thoughtfully. "You," she said sweetly, "look as if you're getting some ideas."

"Oh, I am," he leered. "Why don't you take off that dress, and we'll discuss them?"

Adara felt a throb run down through her core at the thought. She had a few ideas in that direction, herself. But first, to business! "Later, love," she said dismissively, and caught a hint of disappointment in his eyes. "I've been studying up on Kragstein and the Bloodspire during the evenings while I was traveling here," she went on.

Stepping across to where her pack sat atop the dresser, she pulled forth a folded piece of paper from an outside pocket. Ferdyn sat up, his lonely cock momentarily forgotten, and watched with interest as she spread the map out on the table before them. His anxiety to catch Adara had been so great, he'd made none of the preparations he had been intending.

The map showed the region around Kragstein, with Baadzen just visible at the bottom. The mountain fortress was shown in some detail, the surrounding peaks drawn in relief. "Kragstein is a small walled city, really more like a large fortress," Adara explained. "It's built into the side of the mountain, the peak of which is the Bloodspire. It's a natural stone spire, probably what was left after an ancient volcano blew itself apart. The bowl that was left behind became the building site for Kragstein, and the stone spire was partially hollowed out as a citadel. Unless you have wings, the only way inside it is from within the city walls."

Ferdyn traced the spot on the map, which seemed to show a single opening at the base of the tower. "What's its history?" he asked. He had been the teacher as he and Adara traveled halfway across the kingdom from Rivermarch, but in his travels these past eight years he had never been this far north. Adara had done her homework, and he sat ready to learn what she could tell him. It warmed the cockles of her heart.

With a slight smile, she recited what she'd learned. "The place was occupied from ancient times, probably by a series of Nordish warlords." The natives of Nordstan, Tanar's northern neighbor, found cold climates appealing. "Gradually the modern city grew up inside the walls," Adara went on. "There's some herding activity in the mountain meadows nearby, and they grow some hay for winter fodder, but the growing season at that altitude is too short to feed much of a population. The residents mostly supported themselves by mining."

"So, the gold story is true?" Ferdyn asked. Adara shook her head unsurely.

"That part of the Neigande range is rich in iron, hence the red color of the so-called Bloodspire. There were some other minerals found in enough quantity to make mining worthwhile, and there was always some gold to be found in the many mountain streams. But prior to the arrival of Sarand around thirty years ago, there had never been any large quantities of gold coming out of the region."

Ferdyn frowned in concentration, the wheels turning, and Adara watched him in delight. As much as she loved his carefree, fun-loving attitude, his sexual energy, and his fantastically sexy body, his agile mind gave her nearly as big a thrill. She was not disappointed. "Sarand's getting the gold from some other dimension," he said. Adara grinned at him

"I'm sure you're right!" she cried. "Maybe even the same place the Swinzen come from. What's in it for them, I can't imagine. But if we could somehow make it so Sarand can't access that other dimension anymore, his power base will collapse."

Ferdyn nodded enthusiastically, as he tried to figure out how that might be achieved. Since he knew little about magic and had no idea how it was Sarand was able to interact with other dimensions in the first place, that line of thought would have to be tabled. "He took his surname from the fortress he took over," he remarked. "I suppose Sarand's not his real name either…"

"It's the name of an aromatic resin that comes from Khouresh," Adara shrugged. "Nanny kept some of it around for love potions. I suppose if he's Khoureshi that *might* be his real name…" Ferdyn sighed.

"Well, all of that's a moot point I suppose. It looks like we're going to need to show up at the gates of Kragstein with a cartload of root vegetables, if we want to be let inside the walls."

Adara tapped a fingertip on the table, staring into space. It was Ferdyn's turn to gaze at her in admiration. She was so young, so innocent in many ways. But he'd met no one with a finer mind. By the time she was in her thirties, he was sure, she would be the most formidable woman he had ever seen.

"You and I certainly don't look much like farmers," Adara said at last. "And Simdal and Zarhya *really* don't look like cart horses. I suppose we might be able to find some farmer here or in the surrounding area who'd sell us a cart and horse, and some clothing of the kind the local yokels wear. But that would probably be at least a two-day trip up the mountain with a heavy cart, and sleeping out in freezing conditions halfway up. There are no more inns between here and Kragstein."

Ferdyn's eyes lit as a thought came to him. He leaned across the table and explained his idea to Adara, and her own eyes lit. Then he told her about the other idea that was on his mind. She came around the table and sat on his lap, and began unbuttoning his shirt.

Chapter 27

Adara and Ferdyn got a late start leaving Baadzen. After days apart, they hadn't felt they could get out of bed without making love again. Then there'd been a hasty hot breakfast, followed by a tour of the local merchants. But by a little past 9:30 in the morning, they were on their way on the last leg of the journey north.

Kragstein stood at six thousand feet, twice the elevation of Baadzen. The road was paved with stone, else it would have been impassable for much of the year. And it wound up into the mountains by a circuitous path, curving around mountainsides and climbing steep grades by switchbacks.

The two were well bundled-up in woolen underwear beneath their armor, fur cloaks atop it. The brilliantly blue sky held towering white clouds, but it looked unlikely that any snow would fall during their journey. And the mountain scenery *was* truly breathtaking.

They stopped a little past midday, where an icy mountain stream chattered beside a nearly-level stretch of road, and let the horses rest as they sat down on their bedrolls and lunched on bread, cheese, and ham bought this morning from the Maridem's Waters Inn.

They were far from the only traffic on this road, indeed their plan relied on that fact. Coming downhill were occasional farm carts, rattling empty or loaded with chunks of iron ore. Moving much more slowly the other way were farm carts and larger wagons, pulled by heavy draft horses or oxen, hauling loads of root crops, winter vegetables, and grains to feed the populace of Kragstein.

As they passed each of these conveyances, the two riders on their swift desert horses looked them over. "That one was nearly ideal," Adara remarked to Ferdyn as they moved up the road.

"A pity, but it's not getting there until sometime tomorrow," he replied. They kept moving.

As the crow – or perhaps, the eagle – flies, it was not twenty miles from Baadzen to Kragstein. By the road, it was closer to fifty. It wasn't until Adara and Ferdyn had long since spotted the mountain fortress looming above them that they began to take serious consideration of the wagons laboring up the slopes toward it.

When they judged that only a couple more bends stood between them and their goal, the pair pulled their puffing mounts to the side of the road and let them rest. They'd already identified the wagon that was their target, but it would probably not be here for another half an hour. They removed the horses' bridles, replacing them with halters, and tied on feedbags so they could recoup their energies with some grain.

The sun was well down toward the western horizon by the time the wagon they'd chosen came into view around the bend at the bottom of the slope. Her money pouch at her side, Adara stepped out into the road and trotted down toward it. A lone man, in his early twenties, rode the plank that served as a driver's bench on the smallish wagon pulled by a team of horses similar in size (and age) to old Bulo. They were lathered and panting.

"Excuse me, sir!" Adara called, as Ferdyn hung back with Simdal and Zarhya. The young man blinked in astonishment. He'd been curious about the two riders when they'd passed him half an hour earlier, wondering what business they could have in Kragstein. Now, here they were again – and the young woman was even more attractive from the front than she'd been from behind!

Denval drew in on the reins and the horses happily responded to the command to halt. At this point in their long day's labors, they'd have been pleased not to move from that spot for several more hours. "What is it, miss?" he asked, concerned. She looked so young, despite her rough garb.

Adara climbed up and sat beside Denval on the bench, and looked him in the eyes. "Hi," she said. "I'm Elena. Can I ask your name?"

"Um, Denval," he nearly stammered. What was happening here?

"Pleased to meet you, Denval," the vision went on. "So, what's in the cart?"

Denval was nearly poleaxed. He'd been hauling produce along this route for nearly four years, and nothing like this had ever happened. "Beets," he replied shortly. Her eyes seemed to suggest that beets, by the strangest coincidence, were her favorite thing in the world.

"And how much are you hoping to get for your cartload of beets?" Elena went on.

"Um, Uncle expects three marks," Denval managed. Doing a quick assessment, Adara suggested "What if I were to pay you *five* marks?" He goggled at her.

"What, right here? In the middle of the road?" Adara motioned up the road a few yards to where Ferdyn stood beside their horses. Two young Khoureshi horses and their tack were worth more than the cart, its contents, and the animals pulling it, no doubt. But she intended to sweeten the deal.

"My sister was taken by the Mancer King," Adara declared fiercely. "And I have hired a champion to help me get her back. But we must first get inside the walls of Kragstein. I will give you our horses, and a gold mark, so you can return to Baadzen and wait for the return of your cart and horses. When we come back to claim our own horses, we will return yours and give you an additional four marks. You have my word on it."

Thinking with the smaller of his two heads, Denval was lost. It never occurred to him to ask why this beautiful, wealthy (and curiously-dressed) young woman's sister should be living in Kragstein when she – obviously still a teenager – did not. He recognized a pair of Khoureshi horses when he saw them, and knew that if she did not return the cart and the animals pulling it he would still be ahead by at least a couple of marks. "Sure!" he said eagerly, squeezing her hands in sympathy. "Where in Baadzen should I meet you?"

As Denval receded from view, riding Simdal as he led Zarhya around the bend, Adara stifled a sigh. It had gone exactly according to plan, and now it was time for her to get busy with the next part of that plan. Ferdyn was already pulling the rough-spun tunic and trousers on over his armor, making him appear not only rustic but thirty pounds heavier.

It was important that Adara, young and lovely as she was, not appear as a candidate for the Mancer King's sequential harem. Considering the chill as the sun fell toward the western horizon, it was no great burden to layer on more clothing until it appeared she was carrying another fifty pounds. She removed a vial from her pack, plant sap collected before they left Baadzen, and smeared it onto her face. It gave the appearance of years of age, coupled with a scrofulous skin disease.

"Adara my darling, you look absolutely awful!" Ferdyn declared, as the two of them clambered aboard the cart after stowing their packs and weaponry beneath the beets filling its bed. She dimpled at him.

"Why thank you, my dear," she replied sweetly. "And might I say that you look quite bloated and infirm?"

Chapter 28

Sunset was still at least half an hour off as the creaking cart approached the open gates of Kragstein. There was only one entrance. Beyond it, the Bloodspire glinted red in the day's last light. A pair of humans flanked the gate, but standing close behind them was a cohort of Swinzen guards. Adara kept a close rein on her reactions as she beheld them – the armed and armored pig-men who had killed her family. She kept her head down, an expression of exhausted submission on her twisted features.

"You're the last today," the human commander told them. There'd been little in the way of inspection, and their Swinzen overseers didn't seem to be expecting anything beyond the usual. Oddly, Adara was coming to see the pig-man demons as something other than enemies – as much victims of Sarand Bloodspire's evil as she was, as were the human inhabitants of Kragstein.

"Take it over to the Royal Repository," they were commanded, and Ferdyn guided the tired team in that direction. They found themselves approaching the base of the Bloodspire, in which a broad opening gave entry to the evil magus' stronghold. The repository was a two-story stone building beside what seemed to be the spire's only entrance, and he suspected that it served only as a transfer station. Likely Sarand Bloodspire controlled the flow of all supplies in his little kingdom – and all foodstuffs brought in through the gates would soon find their way to some heavily-fortified storehouse within the tower itself.

No one was watching them, and they pulled the cart into a shadowed area south of the tower. Hastily, their packs and armaments were removed from beneath the beets and stowed under a pile of broken furniture and other debris. Wherever humans gathered, there you would find a midden heap.

After the brief detour, the overweight and uncomely farm couple reported to the Royal Repository as ordered. Their beets were unloaded and weighed, and gold – red gold coins, stamped with what they assumed was an image of the Mancer King – was delivered into their hands. Three pieces of it.

They drove the empty cart away, looking for an inn. Though Kragstein was smaller than some of the villages they'd passed through on their separate journeys from King's Crossing, it appeared to have three of them. They settled on the one nearest the spire, and drove the cart around into the stableyard behind it.

The inn was full of farmers and their employees. Who else would need lodging in Kragstein? Adara and Ferdyn hastily partook of what fare was to be had – a stew thick with mutton, turnips, potatoes, and cabbage – and then quickly sought their room. It had been a long day.

Adara tore at her face. "Augh! It burns!" she declared, and Ferdyn looked on sympathetically. They'd retrieved their packs, but had left Virago and Voleur hidden beneath the pile of debris half a block from the inn. Soon Adara had removed the disfiguring sap from her face, but it had left behind a rash. Ferdyn stepped close, enfolding her in his arms, and kissed the red spots.

"Let's pretend we're both thirteen," he suggested cheerfully. She looked up into his eyes.

"Ooh," she said. "Does that mean you have a boner that won't go away?"

Some time later, the two of them lay in each other's arms in the inn room's double bed. "We're in," Ferdyn said. "What's the next part of the plan?" Adara made an effort to gather her thoughts. She was beginning to wonder if she'd been insane not to insist that he stay behind in Baadzen. It had recently occurred to her that the presence of Ferdyn, especially his presence in her bed, had a way of eroding her powers of sound judgment.

"We need to do some reconnaissance," she replied. "But that's going to require daylight." Ferdyn kissed her ear and squeezed her tighter.

She remained silent for a time, then said "You remember I mentioned my powers? I've come up with a new one."

In the morning the farmer's wife turned up poorly, and he fetched breakfast for both of them and brought it back to their room. Adara fell on the freshly baked bread with butter, jam, and bacon as if it were a feast. As soon as they had finished eating, she lay back on the bed.

143

"What do I need to do?" Ferdyn asked worriedly. She'd tried to explain how riding worked last night, but he had never heard of it before – let alone observed it – and he was anxious.

"Just stand by, and watch," Adara told him calmly. "I don't foresee any problems. If the creature I'm riding should die suddenly, I'll be back here with you in an instant and maybe a little upset. Just smother me with kisses, all right?"

He grinned. "That, I can do," he assured her.

Adara lay back on the bed, and in a moment her awareness was questing outward – encompassing the entirety of Kragstein, and everything around it for nearly a mile beyond. The ring's enchantment had given her a mastery it should have taken years to achieve.

The life forces of several dozen humans lit the space within the city's walls. In amid that brightness were many smaller lives. And above the city, birds circled. Adara homed in on a gyrfalcon riding the thermals above the Bloodspire, and pulled it in. While allowing the bird to do what he did best, operating his superb anatomy, she gently overrode his own desires with her own. In the hawk's tiny mind, Adara's aims were his.

The gyrfalcon's vision was sharp, far better than anything human. And the view from up here was spectacular; but Adara resisted the temptation to become lost in it, to give herself over to the joy of flight. The Bloodspire was nearly six hundred feet tall from its base at street level in Kragstein to its crumbling tip. But only the bottom two hundred feet or so, some twelve storeys, had been hollowed out and converted to the uses of man.

The bird circled lower, Adara's mind taking in details. It appeared that the spire must be nearly two hundred feet in diameter at its base, but it tapered sharply as it climbed. Where the windows ended, it was probably no more than thirty feet across – a needle of red stone.

The windows began around three storeys up, offering ventilation. But most of them stood closed, shuttered against the wind and cold. However, the hawk's sharp eyes picked out a window standing open on the very top level. Bidden by Adara, it came in for a landing, perching in the embrasure for a look inside the more-or-less circular tower room.

The room was comfortably furnished, carpets and wall hangings softening the harsh stone, and it reminded Adara quite a lot of Magus Milegos' chamber in the royal palace in Carlienne. There were bits of alchemical apparatus and curious artifacts scattered about, and two more open windows admitting daylight.

A slender man dressed in magus robes stood at a work table. He looked to be no more than forty years old – could this truly be Sarand? His skin was dusky, luxuriant beard and long hair black. The face was cruelly handsome, with a hooked nose and glittering black eyes. Probably a Khoureshi, or a member of one of the eastern desert tribes who fell under the Sultanate's rule.

Adara could not imagine there being any *other* magus occupying the highest room in the Bloodspire, so this must surely be the man she sought – the man who had sent demons to kill her family. The man who would not cease his efforts until he had finally wrested the Darkshield from her. A pity the hawk was not a dragon, so she could just dispatch him now. He stood bent in concentration over a broad, shallow bowl filled with some liquid, and had not noticed the bird's arrival on his window sill.

There probably *were* dragons not that far from here, Adara thought. They preferred these cold mountain climes. But even the smallest dragon would not fit through this window, alas. And if they were sentient, as legend claimed, she would be unable to ride one in any case. As the bird perched silently watching, the magus suddenly broke his concentration and looked up.

Sarand Bloodspire, once Barukh din Aldani, sighed in frustration. After weeks of attempts, he had finally managed to scry the party of Swinzen he had sent after the girl. When he had not found them at first, he had hoped that meant they had her. The Tursaqtam's blinding of his magical sight would have produced such an effect. But there they were, struggling back to Kragstein across many miles of hostile territory in which they must hide by day and move by night – and they were empty-handed. Curses!

That was the problem with the Swinzen, he mused. The very weakness of their mentalities that made them so susceptible to his spells of loyalty and obedience made them less effective as servants. An unenthralled human would perform far better, and those he had employed to locate the girl this time, bound to him by nothing but gold, had been successful. Maybe next time he should hire one of them not only to find the girl, but to overpower her and bring her to him.

Already twenty years had passed since he had first sought the Tursaqtam, had first caught a hint that it still existed. He was determined to have it, and if he had to wait another twenty years so be it. With the magical arts he had learned in his homeland he appeared to be little more than half his true age, and there was yet time for him to fulfill his dream – to rule over the whole of Eorla as emperor.

Then he would have his pick of the most delectable girls, and there would be no need to reduce their minds to quivering jellies – they would besiege him, eager to share his bed, all of their own volition – just to have a taste of his power. Perhaps he would even find one, a woman he would not tire of after a month, a woman with a mind the equal of his own. She would rule beside him, and bear him many fine sons.

Sighing again, Sarand stretched his spine. He'd been bent over the scrying pool for far too long, and his back ached. His glance fell on the gyrfalcon perched on the window ledge, staring at him with its fierce eyes, and he froze. Was the bird injured, that it had come to rest here? The magical ward he had erected to protect the upper levels of the tower from vermin should have repelled it, if it had tried to come inside.

With a gesture and a muttered incantation he cast a spell of calm over the hawk. He would examine it, and make sure that it was truly no more than it seemed: a natural creature. Adara felt a shroud fall over the gyrfalcon's mind, and immediately realized what had happened. The Mancer King had cast a spell on it, probably one intended to render it passive so he could examine it more closely. Her own mind was protected by the Darkshield, and she could have dragged the hawk away. But then, Sarand might wonder why his spell had not worked. Instead, she fled back to her own body and sat up on the bed.

Ferdyn had been seated at the room's small table, reading one of the history books she'd brought along; but as soon as she stirred he was on his feet in an instant and hurried to her side. "Are you all right, darling?" he asked in concern. She smiled at him, drawing an arm across her forehead to wipe away the perspiration. It was not particularly warm in the room, but her close encounter with Sarand had been upsetting.

"I saw the Mancer King," she told him. "He was up in a room at the tower's top level, staring at what looked like a bowl of water."

"Probably some kind of scrying device," Ferdyn suggested, and Adara nodded.

"I need to find some small creature that can get inside the tower, so I can see what the layout is like inside. Just let me take a little break first."

She used the chamberpot, then took a drink from one of their water skins before lying down once more. Ferdyn watched her anxiously as her eyes closed and her spirit once more left her body. Her chest still rose and fell, slowly and gently, or he might have thought her dead. And that thought filled him with the deepest despair. Shaking away the feeling, he returned to his book.

Adara cast her mind out again, into the tower. As she'd hoped, she soon found that the lower levels of it had their share of rats, mice, moths, grain weevils, and spiders. Something small and insignificant would be best. But a spider or a weevil would not be mobile enough, and the fluttering of a moth's wings might draw attention.

She entered a mouse, as she had done on her first recent attempt at riding. Now, though, she had complete and effortless control. The little gray creature stayed close to the juncture of the floor and wall, flowing along silently and almost invisibly on its soft little feet.

She soon discovered that the tower's base, where it met street level in Kragstein, was evidently not the lowest level of the Bloodspire. Double doors flanked by Swinzen guards gave on a broad stone staircase leading down. They must keep their food stores down there, Adara realized. But that was not the direction in which she wanted to go.

Wishing rodents had sharper vision, Adara rode her tiny mount along a corridor. The ground floor had been honeycombed with chambers while leaving much of the native stone intact to provide support for the spire above it. The majority of people she saw were Swinzen – all armed and armored, all apparently male. Unless maybe females of their race looked no different?

She saw more Swinzen emerging from a chamber at the far end, trundling a barrow loaded with small bars of red gold. The treasure room? Though she was not here for treasure, she couldn't resist taking a look. The doorway was flanked by grim-faced guards, but they were not looking for foes at a distance of an inch from the floor. She slipped inside and cowered in the shadow of the iron-bound oaken door where it stood ajar inside the room.

The room was stacked with more of the gold bars, and half a dozen guards were on duty within it. The floor, ceiling, and three walls – including the one with the doorway in it – were of stone. But the fourth wall, at the back of the room! It shimmered like summer sun on a lake, which might turn blue then white then black as a breeze stirred the surface of the waters. Then, as Adara goggled through the mouse's beady eyes, a pair of Swinzen guards pushing a barrow identical to the one she had seen earlier came through the mysterious surface into the room.

A human functionary with a ledger book stepped up and set about counting the bars in the cart. Then he apparently signed off, and the two Swinzen turned on their heels and went back through the wall whence they'd come. Sarand's portal to another universe! He had not just developed the summoner's power to temporarily enlist the aid of extra-dimensional beings, but had somehow created a permanent link between this plane of existence and another – through which he had enslaved or at least conquered and exploited the sentient inhabitants of that alien world!

No *wonder* Sarand had so many demons at his command. There was a whole world full of them on the far side of that portal, and apparently his magical arts enabled him to control them en masse, assuring that he had an unlimited supply of willing servants.

But personal experience and her observation that a human hireling was employed to keep track of gold deliveries suggested to

Adara that the Swinzen, unswervingly loyal as they might be, had some drawbacks as servants. Why had they turned tail and run after knocking Nanny out, instead of lying in wait for Adara's return? Perhaps they were just stupid?

The mouse was getting tired, and Adara let it go about its business as she sought out a rat. There were a lot of stairs in this place, and she needed a creature with more physical reserves. She hoped its larger size would not lead to discovery!

The next three levels of the spire, nearly as broad as the bottom one but tapering as they climbed, were honeycombed with more chambers. Adara saw a lot more humans and fewer Swinzen here. Then as she climbed to the fifth level, she got a jolt of terror from her rat. It was all right one moment, but as she tried to get it to set foot on the next landing it was seized with a violent reluctance to go further. Another magic spell?

Applying the power of her mind, Adara gradually took more and more control until only the rat's autonomic functions and muscle memory were operative. Now she was able to move forward, and found this level to be several orders of magnitude more opulent than had been the ones below it.

The bottom floors must be for the staff, she mused, hiding behind a decorative statue and sniffing the air. The rat's eyesight was no better than the mouse's had been, but its sense of smell was excellent. So these upper levels were the residence of the king and those he deemed worthy to share his quarters with him. Surely, that must be a very short list! This was like no royal court Adara had ever heard of, a captive populace held under control by invaders from another dimension.

There was very little stirring here, and Adara climbed an additional set of steps. Once she'd forced the rat past the magical barrier, there were no further difficulties getting it to move. She wanted to find Sarand's personal quarters, perhaps his private dining room. A rat might well be strong enough to carry a small vial of Nerium extract and poison His Majesty's wine.

The next level was quite a bit smaller. From what Adara remembered of the view from outside the spire, the top several levels were probably little wider than that thirty-foot-in-diameter room where the magus kept his equipment. She ducked behind an elaborately-carved breakfront as a human servant appeared at the head of the stairs, carrying a tray on which sat, from the smells, some hot food. The rat's mind stirred at the odor, its ratty hunger rising and infecting Adara's own mind – though she'd breakfasted quite adequately not two hours before.

Quickly, as the door to one of the level's three chambers was unlocked and opened, Adara scurried to follow the serving man inside. Could this possibly be Sarand's private bedchamber? A man who had no friends might prefer to eat alone.

No, it was not. A lovely young woman, clad in nothing but a silken robe, sat at a medium-sized table staring into space. She looked up as the serving man came into the room, bearing his tray. He set the entire tray on the table, then removed one of the three bowls that sat upon it. The smells told Adara it was a stew containing barley, vegetables, and beef.

The girl looked interested, and eagerly seized the spoon that was handed to her. But before she could dig in, the serving man commanded her, "Stop! You will not eat until I give you permission." Her face fell, then went blank.

"Yes, master," she said in a small voice. "What is your wish?"

A rapacious gleam came into the servant's gaze. "Take off that robe," he said, and the girl did as she was told. Her figure was lush and lovely, though her hair was as dull as her eyes. She stared straight ahead now, waiting for further commands. This must be one of Sarand's "concubines," taken for his pleasure and made docile using his magical arts. Evidently once that had been done to her, anyone – or at least, anyone with authority from the Mancer King – could command her.

Leering now, the servant undid his trousers and pulled out his swelling cock. "Suck on this," he told the girl, and she bent to the task. "That's right, harder, yeah, take it all in!" He pressed down on her head, nearly choking the poor girl, and Adara turned away in disgust. So far, under Ferdyn's tutelage, she had known only pleasure and joy from sex. Now she saw its darker side, a good thing turned ugly.

Adara wanted to leave the rat and flee back to her body, back to Ferdyn's arms. But she had still not found where Sarand ate his meals. The room's door had been left slightly ajar. While the rutting manservant and the enspelled girl had their attention occupied, she slipped back out through it.

She watched the rapist emerge some time later and visit each of the other rooms on this level. Evidently his lusts had been sated, for he lingered only long enough to deliver the bowls of stew before coming back out, tray in hand. Adara was making for the stairs up to the next level when the servant spotted the rat darting across the carpet. "You filthy little bugger!" he exclaimed. "How the hell did *you* get up here?" He dashed forward, cornering the creature against the stairwell. As his booted foot came down, Adara fled.

Chapter 29

Adara sat bolt upright with a strangled cry, and Ferdyn was by her side in a moment. Tears were stinging her eyes, and she buried her face in his shoulder as he held her tenderly. When she had calmed down enough to report what she'd seen, his face became a mask of quiet fury. "We need to get in there and cut that bastard down!" he said emphatically. He'd employed many a trick to obtain sex from women in his long and successful career as a cocksman; but using a spell of coercion was no different from forcible rape. Worse, it raped the mind as well as the body.

"The only openings in the tower big enough to pass a human being are those big double doors at the front," Adara mused. "And those bottom levels are thick with Swinzen guards. Plus there are human hirelings among them, smart enough to penetrate any disguise we might put on."

Ferdyn sat beside her on the bed, his arm around her, and thought. "Maybe I could pretend to be bringing a new sweetmeat for Sarand's harem?" he suggested. Adara shook her head.

"I expect any new girl would be ensconced in one of those locked tower rooms, and they'd be shooing you back out with your pay long before Sarand would come to pay me a visit. Then as soon as he went to cast his spell on me, he'd realize who I was. Besides, I got the idea he prefers them shorter and a little, uh, meatier than I am."

"You said that there are lots of human servants?" Ferdyn asked next. "Could we maybe get into the fortress on the pretense of looking for work?"

"I doubt we'd get much above the first level, if they would even let us in the door," she replied. "It's a pity Sarand doesn't have servants that come in for the day and go home at night, but from what I saw everyone who works there is quartered on the lower levels of the spire."

Adara furrowed her brow, trying to force her brain into coming up with a solution. Kill everyone in the spire with poisoned meat? Call Nomen to shake the earth until the spire fell? That last one would probably work, she realized – but it would also probably flatten half of Kragstein in the process, and kill many people who were guilty of nothing more awful than being under the thrall of the evil magus.

"I could show up at the front door with the Darkshield clearly visible and announce that I'd come to give myself willingly to Sarand," Adara suggested. "He'd probably be so overjoyed he wouldn't be on his guard, and I could stab him with a poisoned dagger while he was gloating over my submission."

"Yeah, and then his loyal Swinzen guards would probably hack you limb from limb for killing their boss, before rampaging out into Tanar," Ferdyn objected. "You're not going to be able to go in there wearing Voleur, and that means you'll need me there to handle the soldiers."

Adara wasn't certain that would be the outcome. From what she had sensed of the many Swinzen she'd seen inside the spire, they were as enspelled as that poor girl had been. Might they not welcome the chance to return to their homes? But on the other hand, there was a chance Ferdyn was right. Even with Salomand at her call, without weapons or armor she would be unable to fight off the hordes of guards within the spire. And if she succeeded in killing Sarand when no guards were around, how could she make her way down all those levels to escape the tower?

"Since I was unable to find Sarand's living quarters," Adara said, "I think it would be better if we could lure him down to the bottom of the tower. What about if you pretend to be a freebooting mercenary, who's heard Sarand was looking for me and decided to take me captive and bring me to sell to him? You're looking for a big payoff, I'm subdued but hate you with a passion, then you pull Virago and take off his head while he's counting out the money and we fight our way out the door to freedom. What do you think of that?"

Ferdyn sighed. He really, really didn't like the idea of pretending to sell his beloved to her worst enemy. But he was running out of ideas. "We should have thought of that yesterday," he said. "We could have saved all that foolishness with the beets. As it is, how are we to get away from here once we break free of the spire?"

"Why, we just sneak back into our inn room. There's a door down at the end of the hall that leads to the stableyard. We lie low, and in the morning we're just Mister and Mistress Hayseed, taking our cart back to the farm."

"We're going to do this at night, then?" Ferdyn asked. He seemed to be buying into the idea, and Adara wished it were a better one.

"This evening, just before they close the spire gates for the night," she suggested. "Things are pretty busy around the front of the spire at that point, and you'll refuse to bring your captive inside until the boss man is brought to promise you payment. That ought to get Sarand downstairs. If we could lure him out into the street even better, but I doubt he'd set foot outside the tower without being well-warded against harm."

"All right, that's what we'll do then," Ferdyn said, leaning back against the head of the bed. "We'll gather our clothes and equipment after supper. But *how* shall we pass the time in the meanwhile?" His burning gaze left no doubt how *he* would like to spend that time, and Adara was in accord with him. She crawled up the bed and into his arms, her hand stroking his thigh.

Chapter 30

All was in readiness, and as dusk was falling the rakish freebooter and his hapless captive slipped out the inn's rear doorway and into the gathering gloom. The front entrance of the Bloodspire was brightly lit with torches, and a line of wagons was backed up beside the next-door Royal Repository. For the heavier wagons, the trip between Baadzen and Kragstein was a long two days.

Adara's long hair had been braided into a queue behind her back, her hands bound likewise, and Ferdyn held her by the braid as he chivvied her along. Her head was down, eyes furious, stumbling in the near-darkness as they approached the gates of the tower.

They were guarded by half a dozen Swinzen, and the one nearest the right side of the opening commanded, "Halt!" So, they did speak Franca after all – or at least, some of them did. It stood to reason that they must, else how could they keep the human citizens of Kragstein in line? But even while she was spying inside the tower earlier today, she had not heard them speak in anything but their own tongue.

"Only authorized personnel are allowed inside the Bloodspire," the Swinzen captain announced. He had a guttural accent, and those tusks gave him quite a lisp. But he was able to make himself understood. Ferdyn, half a foot taller than the porcine guard, said haughtily, "Get your boss out here – whatsisname, the Mancer King. He's going to want to authorize *me* when he finds out who I've got here."

The piggy little eyes regarded him impassively. "And who are you?" the guard asked. "None other than Ferdyn Longblade, plunderer of ancient tombs and performer of legendary feats!" Ferdyn boasted. He'd carved his facial hair into something a little more elaborate and waxed it, making him look like a bit of a fop. In addition, he'd added a scarlet scarf to his ensemble. He was going for piratical, but that was hard to pull off with his smooth, unscarred face and light complexion.

"I happened across this little sweetmeat here," Ferdyn went on, nudging Adara. She staggered slightly and glared at him. "And I heard the Mancer King was looking for her. I thought I'd save him the trouble of going out and finding her himself, so I brought her along. I expect there'll be quite a reward offered for *this*!" He yanked at the opening of her blouse, ripping off a couple of buttons, and fingered the Darkshield where it lay across her collarbone. The guard's eyes widened.

"Stay here," he commanded. Ferdyn grinned at him, the kind of expression that might have made a fellow human want to belt him in the nose. It didn't appear to have that effect on the Swinzen, whether because they didn't respond to human facial expressions or because of the enchantment they were under.

The guard captain barked an order to an underling in his harsh, grunting language and the younger demon saluted and dashed off – into the spire and away. Yes, just as they'd hoped. While they waited for a response from the message that had been sent, the captain asked "Where did you find her?" He personally knew several of the members of the squad sent to capture the Tursaqtam bearer, and was curious. Sarand's loyalty spell did not prevent him from thinking for himself.

"She was fleeing along the road from Pine Hill to Grandwyl in Rivermarch," Ferdyn answered truthfully. "All by herself on an old plough horse, a helpless girl. I was going to have her on the spot, but when I got the blouse off I discovered the necklace there. I'd heard about it, and I knew right away she was worth a lot more than a quick lay." Adara's disgruntlement was not entirely feigned.

In his seventh level dining room, Sarand Bloodspire was finishing another excellent dinner. His spells allowed him to eat as much as he cared to without becoming fat, and over the years gourmet delicacies had become one of his main pleasures in life. The difficulty of obtaining them in this remote mountain fastness only enhanced their appeal.

The girls were another, but truly they were good for fucking and nothing else. Oh, what he would not give for a boon companion, someone to converse with at the table! He had dined alone for most of the time since taking over the Bloodspire and its surrounding fortress, having no one whose company was worth enjoying.

Sarand looked up, dark eyes glittering, as one of the Swinzen guards came into the room. The squat little monstrosity was panting with exertion, and must have run all the way up the six flights of stairs from the ground floor. He frowned in annoyance. Loyal and obedient the Swinzen might be, yet somehow he could never completely get across that he did *not* want to see their kind on the upper levels of the spire.

"What is it?" he snapped, and the young demon guard quailed. He snapped a quick salute, hoping to escape the master's wrath. Some of his fellows had been roasted on the spot when the Mancer King had found their performance wanting.

"Sir!" the young guard reported. "Captain Dzeragh ordered me to inform you that there is a mercenary at the gates. He appears to have in his possession the young woman bearing the Tursaqtam, and the captain requests that you come to the gates so this can be verified."

Sarand rose to his feet in an instant, tossing his napkin aside. This morning he had idly considered hiring human mercenaries to capture the girl, and a few hours later one appears at the gates with her in hand? The *djinni* must have smiled upon him! He brushed aside his annoyance at the swinish intrusion, and accompanied the young guard back down the stairs.

All the way down the six flights of steps the young Swinzen guard was praying to his own gods – the gods of his people back in his home universe – that this human woman, and the necklace she bore, were genuine. He did not fancy his chances for survival, or those of the rest of his troop, if she turned out to be a hoax.

Captain Dzeragh looked up with relief as he saw Private Haughnz coming down the corridor accompanied by the Master. The Mancer King looked excited, not angry, and he only hoped that meant he was not to be punished for sending the private up to the seventh level. As a general rule, none of the Swinzen (as the strange natives of this dimension insisted on calling his people) were permitted to climb higher than the fourth floor.

The necklace was displayed again in the torchlight, and Sarand beckoned for the mercenary and his captive to be brought inside. Private Haughnz rejoined his squad, and the Mancer King commanded the captain to round up another group of guards to accompany them to an unused chamber on this floor. At this hour the ground floor of the Bloodspire was chaotic, and he wanted some peace and quiet – and also, some security.

The tall mercenary was swaggering, quite pleased with himself, as he and his captive were led into a smallish chamber that gave off the ground floor's central corridor. Clearly, he thought he had just cashed in on the score of a lifetime. Excitement was rising as Sarand's eyes kept returning to the girl. She was beautiful, far more so than his agent's description had prepared him for. Too tall and too thin for his usual taste, but despite being in bondage she had a certain fire he found appealing. But the final test would come in just a moment, as soon as the door of the chamber had been closed.

Chapter 31

The six of them stood in a circle around the small chamber. Sarand was keeping a careful eye on the mercenary, who looked like he might be a dangerous fellow; but most of his attention was taken up by the girl. Was it really her? "What is your name, girl?" he commanded – though the answer was of little importance.

She drew herself up, clearly not defeated. "Adara Willoughby," she said coldly. A small smile reached no further than Sarand's eyes, as he cast a lethal spell. If she were unprotected, her heart would simply stop beating. Adara's startling blue eyes widened as she felt the Darkshield grow warm, its central gem sending out a pulse of red light. Her heart did not stop.

Yes, finally! Sarand exulted silently. His attention turned to Ferdyn, and caught him with Virago halfway out of her scabbard. Treachery? In an instant Ferdyn collapsed to the floor, felled by a spell of sleep. He would awaken shortly, but it would not avail him. "Disarm him and throw him into the dungeon," Sarand commanded. "I will deal with him later!"

The entire force of Swinzen guards, galvanized into action by the master's command, hauled Ferdyn up from where he lay on the floor and carried him away through the door. The tower's small dungeon, as well as its storerooms, had been carved into the rock of the mountain below.

Oh fucking shit, Adara thought. Time for Plan B. It was reasonably safe to assume that Ferdyn was not yet dead, and she carefully showed no outward signs of distress at his felling. "Tell them to cut out his liver, while they're at it!" she spat. The magus turned to her, a smile wreathing his handsome features at this sign of her unquenched spirit.

"We meet at last, my dear," he said in slightly accented Franca. As he had been resident in this part of Eorla for far longer than Adara had been alive, it was not surprising that he had a good command of the tongue.

"I don't believe we've actually been introduced," the girl pointed out.

"My apologies," Sarand said suavely. "My name is Sarand Bloodspire, but you may call me 'master.'" Adara drew herself up.

"I believe I would prefer to call you Sarand," she said. He raised an eyebrow. The man was quite devilishly handsome, in a dark sort of way.

"You want the Darkshield," Adara continued boldly. "With it, you will be safe from any magus who might seek to stop you. Once you have it, you will rule over Tanar." She hesitated, gauging his response. "And then, perhaps," she went on, "over all of Eorla?"

Yes, that *was* his intention, Adara realized. What a megalomaniac! Why anyone would seek to have such power was beyond her. It would surely be nothing but a giant headache trying to administer the government of thousands of square miles, containing millions of cantankerous and contrary human beings. But in her role as a young woman seeking power, she smiled at him beguilingly. "Such ambition excites me," she said. She sensed that she was not his type, but she also sensed a hint of… loneliness? This so-very-powerful man must have lived a large part of his life without anyone to call a close friend. Might she be that friend?

Sarand was both taken aback and excited. He had spent hours, years, imagining how he would get the bearer of the Tursaqtam to place it around his own neck – torture, threats to a loved one… It had not really occurred to him that she might give it to him freely – eager to partake of the power he anticipated would be his. But she *was*, after all, a young woman – his target audience. Why not?

The overly-tall and somewhat scrawny young Adara's allure had just risen sharply. Sarand stepped closer. But he stopped while he was still out of range. "You would give the Tursaqtam, the Darkshield as you call it, to me willingly?"

"The Darkshield has been passed in a continuous chain of love since it was created by Astrinda millennia ago. Were you my love, I should be happy to give it to you," Adara purred. Ferdyn *was* her love, or at least as much of a love as she had in her life, and she had not been willing to hand it over to him. But she must convince Sarand that, if he but made an effort to win her, she and the priceless magical artifact she bore could both be his.

160

It was so tempting! But Barukh was more than seventy years old. And while the enticement of the female still motivated him, thanks to the age-suppressing effects of his arts, he had the wisdom that went with his years. It made him cautious. "You are beautiful, Adara," he said smoothly. "I think it possible that I could come to love you. Could you ever love me?"

She gazed into his eyes, which were at a height with hers. Her own were wide, blue, and guileless. "You are a fine figure of a man, my lord," she replied. She did not go so far as to acknowledge his claim to royalty. "Handsome, wise, and possessed of great powers. Were you to find *me* someone with whom you could share these powers, I think we might be happy together."

Sarand blinked. "You are yet a maiden?" he asked. Such considerations had not bothered him before, but if he was to take a consort – a woman who would stay by his side – his male pride demanded that he be the first and only man to share her bed. Adara dropped her eyes, wishing she could produce a blush on demand.

"That filthy pig who captured me on the road from Pine Hill intended to rape me," she admitted. "But he stayed his… hand, when he saw the Darkshield. I remain unsullied."

The magus' interest was piqued. She was lovely, if not his preferred physical type. And had he not been longing to find a woman who would come to him willingly, whose mind would remain intact? He must test her resolve, and he stepped closer. "I must know if you truly want me, Adara," he said. "Will you give yourself to me, here and now?"

Adara cast down her eyes again, shy. "I… oh, I do want you! But I don't know what to do…" She was replaying some scenes from the past month, when she had given herself to Ferdyn. But now, she must tamp down all the horror, all the revulsion she felt. Only her maidenly reserve must show through.

A sardonic smile came across Sarand's handsome face, as his suppressed excitement – and his cock – began to rise. "I will guide you, my dear," he said softly… stepping behind her and cutting through her bonds with the dagger he kept about his person. He'd been cutting meat with it not half an hour ago. In another moment he stood in front of her again.

"Start by removing your clothes." After rubbing at her wrists to restore circulation Adara quailed, but then peered out at him from beneath her lashes.

"All right," she said in a small voice. Thank Maridem she had decided *not* to secrete a few daggers about her person! The plan had been for Ferdyn to behead the Mancer King during the first few minutes of their confrontation, after which they would fight their way back out into the city and melt into the shadows. *Why* had it not occurred to them that the magus could paralyze Ferdyn with a thought? It should have been *her* carrying all the heavy armament...

Adara began to strip. Slowly, sensuously, but without any apparent consciousness of her effect on her audience. She was constrained and shy, and undressed in the same order – and the same manner – as she would have if she'd been disrobing for bed. Sarand was eating it up with a spoon, and even with his loosely-fitting robes she could detect his erection.

In minutes she stood naked before him. Her figure was slim, not nearly as curvy as the many concubines who had filled his bed over the past decades. But her youth, and the beauty of her face, were coupled with the fact that she still possessed her whole mind – and wanted him anyway.

Adara crouched at first, as if ashamed and embarrassed. But then she straightened up and looked at Sarand with her hands at her sides, palms up. She seemed to say, "Here I am. Will you have me?" His mind still had reservations, but the old magus' body was beginning to take control. He gazed at her avidly, drinking in her innocence. Or so he imagined it to be.

"My lord," Adara asked softly. "Will you show yourself to me? I hunger for a sight of you in your full glory." How could he decline? The girl was naked, and possessed no weaponry. She wore nothing now but the necklace, the Tursaqtam he had desired since first learning that it still existed. Sarand began to strip.

Adara was surprised that he began with his boots. Beneath the exotic-looking robes that were a mark of his status as a magus, Sarand wore almost a complete suit of ordinary clothing. Next to emerge from the robe's hem was a pair of trousers, and she was hard put not to laugh. How long had it *been*, since this powerful and deadly man had gotten naked with a woman who was not bespelled?

Eventually the robe came off over Sarand's head, to reveal slimly muscled legs, dark skin heavily covered in black body hair, and a towering (if somewhat smaller than Ferdyn's) erection. In another moment the Mancer King had shucked off the long-sleeved wool knit shirt he wore and stood before Adara as naked as she was. He had a jeweled pendant on a gold chain around his neck, and laid it carefully atop the pile of discarded clothing before turning to her again. She schooled her face to show a delicate combination of desire and maidenly awe. Such a thing, that stiff cock! Oh, what *would* she do with it?

Now that the two stood unclothed, facing one another, it was dawning on both of them that this stone-walled chamber in which they stood was eminently unsuited for sexual liaisons. There was no bed, not so much as a carpet on the floor! "My lord?" Adara asked tremulously.

Sarand looked around, annoyed. He was ready, beyond ready. There was no way he intended to re-clothe himself and adjourn to a more suitable boudoir. "Against the wall," he suggested. When she looked at him in consternation he promised, "I'll be gentle."

Adara could vividly imagine. She backed up against the wall and put her hands up behind her head. With quick fingers, she dug into her braid and removed the vial of Nerium extract that had been woven into it. A stout needle had been embedded eye-first in the inner side of its cork-tipped glass stopper.

Sarand approached her, taking in her look of anxiety with pleasure. Quail before my mighty rod, child, he thought as he stepped closer to pin her to the wall. As they were the same height, it was easy for his cock to find the warm haven of her cunt. He began pressing forward eagerly, and as he did Adara threw her arms around his shoulders and sank the poisoned needle an inch deep into his neck. Then she called Salomand, and wriggled out of the way.

Chapter 32

Ferdyn came to consciousness to find himself lying on a floor of cold, hard stone. He was somewhat surprised to discover that he was still wearing his armor. Virago was gone, and so was the long dagger he'd worn at his belt. But the other four daggers he'd secreted about his person, he found, were still there. So were the lockpicks he kept in an inner pocket of the tunic he wore beneath his hauberk. What the hell had happened?

He'd been about to separate the Mancer King from his head, he recalled, as Sarand Bloodspire's attention was focused on Adara. And then what? Try as he might, he could not recall anything. But he was here and Adara was not, and that meant Adara was in danger!

Ferdyn could hear voices down the corridor, voices speaking in the guttural, grunting language of the Swinzen. But no one was near enough to see him as he pulled out the lockpicks and began attacking the lock on the iron door fronting his cell.

The lock was nothing special, and in less than two minutes it yielded with a metallic "clink." Ferdyn swung the door open, alert to the possibility of creaking hinges; but it proved silent. Then he stole down the corridor on his soft boots, a dagger in each hand, and peered around to the left.

He must be in a dungeon below the Bloodspire, he realized. The torchlit room before him held a single round table with four chairs around it, and seated in those chairs were Swinzen guards. They were playing at dice. This was not the first time Ferdyn had found himself in such a place; for while he'd always tried to stay on the right side of the law, there had been times when the law had not stayed on the right side of *him*.

On the far side of the room, he beheld a sight that filled him with hope: his missing weapons, leaning up against the stone wall. Hard to get good help, ain't it, Sarand? Ferdyn thought as he threw the two daggers in his hands. Each of them took one of the Swinzen guards on the far side of the table in the neck, and as their companions rose from their seats in horror he swept into them, hooking an arm around each guard's neck and bringing their heads hard together.

By the time the stunned guards had recovered themselves enough to draw weapons, Ferdyn had Virago in both hands. A few seconds later, the living population of the guardroom had been reduced to one. He stepped cautiously through the door, and looked out on a much larger room. It was occupied by twenty or more Swinzen guards.

Adara, forgive me! Ferdyn thought as he stepped through the door and began swinging his sword. I tried! Virago singing, he advanced on the massed demons. He had the advantage of surprise, but that was only effective with the first half dozen or so. The rest massed behind them, axes and swords at the ready. Behind them, there were shouts and cries as more were called to corral the escaping prisoner.

Ferdyn overtopped most of the Swinzen by half a foot or more, and with Virago in his hands he was nearly invincible. If only there weren't so damn *many* of them! He strode forward, swinging the blade, and the pig-men fell before him. Could he actually triumph? Adara, I'm coming! Then reinforcements appeared at the back of the room. Reinforcements with drawn bows.

Oh, shit. Ferdyn let his blade fall at his side as he realized he was done. "Put down the weapon," someone in authority commanded in lisping, guttural accents. "The master commanded you are to be held until he comes." They didn't mean to kill him! Maybe the bowmen would hold their fire, blindly obeying the magically-enforced orders they had last received. He lifted the sword again, prepared to fight his way to Adara's side or die trying.

Suddenly one of the bowmen lowered his weapon, crying out "Dim zei!" He threw his bow to the floor, and vanished into the corridor beyond. "Zei! Zei!" A chorus of voices echoed the cry, as weapons clattered to the stones.

The voice of the officer who had spoken earlier declared, "The master is dead. We are free!" He too threw his weapon down, and left the room.

Stunned, Ferdyn followed him out, walking down the corridor and up a flight of stairs behind a crowd of Swinzen guards who were rushing forward as if the object of their fondest desires was to be found beyond the double doors at the top.

Chapter 33

Sarand Bloodspire's long black hair and beard had burned away, leaving the skin blistered and charred. But it had been the Nerium that killed him, in the end. Adara hastened to get back into her clothing. Would the room soon be swarming with angry Swinzen guards, anxious to chop her into dog meat for the crime of slaying their master?

After she was fully dressed she put an ear to the door, trying to learn what was going on out there in the corridor beyond it. There was a sound as of many feet, and cries in the Swinzen language that meant nothing to her. Oh, if only the door to this disused storeroom had a bar on the inside!

Wait, the deceased Mancer King had used a dagger to free her hands earlier. A fatal mistake, that had proven to be. As a magic user, he might have been accustomed to go about unarmed except for the small knife used to cut his meat. But there might be something else, if only a key she could use to lock this door. As Adara was rummaging through the magus' pile of discarded clothing, the door flew open.

"Adara!" Ferdyn cried. Against her every expectation he was clad in his armor, bearing Virago, and seemingly unharmed. She flew to his arms.

"Ferdyn, oh Ferdyn!" she sobbed. "I thought you were lost!"

"And I you," he said into the top of her head. He had spotted the body of the Mancer King lying on the floor, his head a smoking ruin.

The fact that the corpse was naked had not escaped his notice. "Did he… did you…?" he asked, looking into Adara's eyes in horror.

"In his fucking dreams!" she replied. "I had him all ready to take my 'virginity' standing up against yon wall. But things didn't work out quite like he'd hoped."

He hugged her again. "I was wrong," he told her. "The Swinzen's loyalty apparently evaporated when Sarand died. They all threw down their weapons and ran off saying 'I'm free!'" Adara smiled brilliantly at him. The news was a huge relief. All they had to do was give the formerly-enthralled soldiers time to make their way home… But what if the portal had vanished with the man who had, she presumed, created it?

"The room with the portal to the Swinzen's universe is down at the end of the hall," Adara said tensely. "If the portal's gone, our world is going to have to deal with a couple thousand illegal immigrants…" They both went to the door and listened at it. There were no tramping feet, no guttural shouts. Had the guards all gone?

Ferdyn risked cracking the door and peering down the corridor. It remained deserted. "I think the portal must have persisted after Sarand's death," he told Adara quietly. He opened the door the rest of the way. "Wait, let me see if I can find Sarand's dagger," she said and returned to rifling through the late magus' belongings.

Adara had already pocketed that necklace. From the runes engraved on the pendant, she guessed it had magical properties. As she lifted the voluminous robe, she sensed that something was hidden within it. Turning the garment inside-out, she discovered a number of cunningly-hidden pockets. Here was a small ring of keys, there a lethal-looking black dagger. She took both items, tucking the dagger into her belt.

Meanwhile Ferdyn had been keeping an eye on the corridor, which was still deserted. It appeared that all of the Swinzen guards had fled. But where were the human servants? "You saw a lot of human servants when you were riding your rat?" he asked Adara.

"Most of them were on the floors above here," she replied. "From what I saw of his concubines, the spell he used to command obedience renders the subject as intelligent as a small child. It's likely most of those serving him were not enspelled, so they're probably not aware that Sarand is dead. None I saw were armed with anything more than a dagger for cutting meat, in any case."

Ferdyn nodded. "Well then, shall we explore?" Adara nodded back, and the two of them crept out into the corridor. It was eerily quiet. Down at the far end of it, the door to the room with the portal stood open. Cautiously they made their way to it, and stood stunned. The portal yet existed, which was not a surprise since the Swinzen had to have gone somewhere. What amazed them was that the room was still stacked high with bars of gleaming red gold.

The pair stood there, eyes wide, then exchanged a glance. Both of them were beginning to grin like maniacs. Apparently there really *was* a large reward for bringing Adara to the Bloodspire! "It appears the Swinzen were so eager to return home that they didn't stop to collect their gold," Ferdyn remarked.

"Maybe gold in their world is as common as iron in ours," Adara suggested.

"Could be," he replied. "But I'd prefer not to chance it – that, or the demons deciding to mount an expedition here for revenge on humankind. We need to get this portal closed, somehow." Adara went around the room, examining the walls. There was no sign of a switch, nor did lifting the still-burning lamps from the walls trigger anything.

"The fact that the portal didn't collapse when the rest of Sarand's magic did suggests that it was the result of a device of some sort, not a spell he'd cast," Adara opined.

"I've never heard of any magus with the innate power to create a permanent portal to another world," Ferdyn added. "Most who have dealings with the other planes just temporarily summon creatures from them to do their bidding, from what I've been told."

Adara had a thought, and took from her pocket the necklace Sarand had worn. Assuming the existence of such a magical artifact, and the portal's importance to his ambitions in this dimension, might he not keep such a thing close? He had worn no rings or other jewelry. "This might be the device," she said, holding it up. The stone set amidst the markings mimicked the portal's appearance, appearing first one color and then another. "I could try smashing the jewel with a hammer. That might shut the portal off."

"Or make it so it could never be closed again," Ferdyn warned anxiously. "Why don't you try to wear it, instead? Your ability with riding might enable you to sense the method of its operation." Adara gave him a little smile of thanks and slipped the gold chain on over her head. Huh, would the effect of the Darkshield make it impossible for her to use a necklace with a different effect? Probably not, she assumed. It was not as if she was using the pendant to cast a spell on herself.

"Give me your arm," Adara requested. "I've never tried this standing up before." Ferdyn stepped quickly to her side, giving her a little squeeze, and then stood beside her – ready to hold her up if she should start to fall. With a little squeeze back, she pretended that the pendant hanging from the chain around her neck was a small creature she intended to ride, and sent a part of her consciousness questing within. At the same time, she tried to remain aware of her surroundings and in control of her body.

Yes, it was working! The pendant, crafted who-knew-how-many centuries or millennia ago, seemed almost to have a consciousness of its own. Was it possible for a magus of great power to infuse such artifacts with a part of their souls? Rather than attempting to take it over, imposing her will on it as she would with a mouse, Adara reached out to communicate with it – as she might beseech one of the elementals for a favor.

"Who are you?" Adara asked silently, and the answer came back *"I am Fatiha Baba."* "Can you close the portal I see before me?" she asked next, and Fatiha Baba replied, *"You wear the necklace, so I must obey your command."* With that the portal popped out of existence, leaving nothing but a stone wall on the far side of the chamber!

Wow, Adara thought, and leaned against Ferdyn as a wave of dizziness swept over her. It was not the strain of having her mind in two places at once, so much as her awe at the power she now wore around her neck. Might Fatiha Baba be a key to traveling the dimensions, going where and when she pleased? She was almost afraid to consider it.

Ferdyn seized her in a bear hug. "You did it!" he crowed. "Now we just have to figure out how to keep the spire's human residents from coming down here and raiding the stash before we can get it moved out of here." Adara considered. The door was quite sturdy, and had a pretty impressive-looking lock on it. She dug Sarand's keys out of her pocket and tried them, one at a time. None fit.

"I suppose locking and unlocking this door must have been the responsibility of the Swinzen guards," Adara mused. "Do you think they would have kept the key in their guardroom, or whatever?"

"Let's go see, shall we?" Ferdyn replied, and led the way to the lower level.

"Whoa," she remarked mildly on seeing the carnage below. More than a dozen of the Swinzen guards lay in pools of blood in the larger of the two guardrooms.

Ferdyn glanced down at her dress and light boots. "You wait here, love. I'll search for the keys." He began picking his way among the bodies, searching for a nail on which keys might be hung. There was none, neither here nor in the smaller room beyond where the four had sat playing at dice. The stench in the area was impressive, the Swinzen not smelling good to human nostrils at the best of times. Releasing their sphincters in death had not improved their odor any.

If I were a closely-guarded set of keys to the treasure room and portal, where would I be, he thought – spinning around to study the walls of the room. They'd just leaned his confiscated weapons up against the wall, as there was nothing resembling a lock-up down here. If there had been, the outcome tonight might not have been so favorable.

While he was thinking about the problem, Ferdyn recovered the long dagger the guards had taken and hung it on his hip, also reclaiming Virago's harness and sheathing the sword. Then he turned his attention to the bodies of the guards, retrieving his expertly-thrown daggers. His ability with these had come through many long hours of practice, no magical enhancement needed.

Hmm, he thought, looking at the bodies more closely. This one fellow looked older, and his uniform was different. The Swinzen troops' armor was little different from what he himself wore, and each had a high collar with what he took to be insignia of rank on the lapels. Might this, um, demon, have been the commanding officer? It was worth a try…

Adara was breathing through her mouth and trying to imagine she was elsewhere when Ferdyn returned, picking his way across the floor of the corpse-strewn room to stand at her side. He was jingling an iron ring on which were half a dozen large keys.

Back upstairs, glad to be out of the miasma, they closed the doors leading to the lower level. One of the keys on the ring locked them, leaving no further sign of Swinzen in the tower. Next they went to the treasure room, portal room no more, and tried the largest and most intricate of the keys in its massive lock. It clicked shut!

"Come with me," Adara said, leading the way down to the far end of the hall where the tower's doors still stood open to the night. The populace of Kragstein must be cowed indeed, that no one had come in to investigate during the hour or so since all of the guards had fled.

They pulled the doors shut, and found that another of the Swinzen commander's keys worked to lock them. "Great!" Adara said, smiling. "Let me out, love, and hold the fort while I go back to the inn. I want my armor and weapons before we go upstairs."

Chapter 34

They bypassed the staff quarters to begin with, climbing the stairs all the way to Sarand's twelfth-floor workshop. Adara had brought along both their packs, and they loaded them up with any small items that looked useful or valuable. Hey, to the victor go the spoils.

They found the levels between the seventh and the twelfth essentially empty, not even furnished. Sarand had truly been a lonely man, Adara thought, sparing a split-second of sympathy for him though she did not at all regret having ended his life. The seventh floor was given over to the late magus' personal quarters, which included an enormous bedchamber, study, bathroom and privy chamber, and a small private dining room where the remnants of Sarand's last meal still sat on the polished ebony table.

More small items went into their packs, then the two raiders moved on and down. On the sixth level they could hear loud pounding at the doors of the chambers where the three concubines had been housed. "Let me out! Hello, is anyone there?" could be heard coming from behind the locked doors.

Adara pulled out the small key-ring she'd taken from Sarand and tried it first at the chamber where she'd witnessed the serving man further degrading the bespelled captive within. The door flew open and the young woman, still wearing the robe she'd been in earlier, stood there wide-eyed. There was no doubt from her expression that her mind had been restored when Sarand's spell dissolved.

"Who are you?" she gasped, pulling the robe tighter around her and cringing back into the room. The pair of them, in their well-worn armor and with sword hilts above their shoulders, did look a bit intimidating. Adara put on her warmest smile. After all, this girl was only a couple of years older than she was.

"I'm Adara and this is my friend Ferdyn," she told her. "We've killed Sarand Bloodspire, and the Swinzen guards have all returned to their own world. The portal is closed, so they cannot return. You are now free," she added, in case that wasn't plain.

The young woman's face went from disbelief to joy, to determination and anger, all in the course of a few seconds. "I hope you gutted him like the pig he was," she said through gritted teeth. "What of the human servants here? I have a few other scores to settle." Hmm, it would appear that the captive's mind had not been as far gone as Adara had assumed, watching her service the man who brought her meals. She must have memories, though surely hazy ones, of all that befell her when she had been enthralled.

"Come with us, and we'll be going down to talk with the staff in just a few minutes," Adara suggested. "I'm sorry, I wish I had some clothes for you to put on."

"I know where to get some," the girl replied. "I had been hired to work in the kitchens when the master saw me and decided to make me his plaything." Her lip curled as she said it.

They let the occupants out of the other two rooms, and there were joyful reunions as the three robe-clad girls met again and began trading stories. One was blonde, one redhead, and one as dark as any Khoureshi; but the three had been cast from the same short, buxom mold. No wonder her seduction of the goatish old magus had required such effort, Adara mused.

The party of five now went down two flights of stairs, past the untenanted fifth level to the top level of staff quarters on the fourth floor. The blonde, whose name was Gudrun, told them in a voice seething with resentment, "The rats, mice, and roaches start here. Our illustrious 'master' could just as easily have excluded vermin from the entire tower, but he thought it was more fitting that we common folk not receive the benefit of his warding spell."

She seemed to be the boldest and most outspoken of the three formerly-enthralled concubines, and it was she who led them down the hall to a door behind which, she said, the kitchen staff had their quarters. The kitchen itself was on the second floor, since the majority of those who had needed feeding were the Swinzen troops.

"They always locked us in at night, usually right after we'd had our supper," Gudrun said. "There was a squad of those foul demons who would come through, and if you were caught outside your quarters at closing time Maridem help you. They were mean little bastards."

The door was not locked. Probably all of the Swinzen had abandoned their duties and hightailed it for home before the hour at which that chore would normally be performed – but the well-trained staff would not have noticed. Inside the apartment, a series of doorless rooms had been carved from the red stone. They found a group of women, aged between fourteen and fifty, occupying a single large room at the rear – mostly just talking together in the dim lamplight.

The eldest of these, a woman who from her looks was of Nordish extraction, looked up as they came inside and cried "Gudrun! What…?" The blonde girl ran across the room and threw herself into the well-upholstered older woman's strong arms.

"Hildy, Sarand Bloodspire is dead!" she cried jubilantly. "I'm free!" Every woman in the room jumped to her feet and mobbed their returning colleague, creating a din as their questions and exclamations echoed from the low stone walls of the chamber.

Adara stood aside for a while, watching the touching reunion. Then she spoke up. "Ladies, all of the Swinzen guards have fled through the portal back to their home world. As Sarand is no more, all of his enchantments are at an end. I imagine that most of you were working here under duress?"

Hildy, the chief cook as it happened, spoke for the group. "When Sarand arrived here thirty years ago, the tower stood empty," she said. "Most people in Kragstein made a living working the iron and copper mines, or panning gold from the streams. Then suddenly we found that Sarand had taken over the Bloodspire, and he was backed by a force of those demon troops larger than the entire population of our little town. If he wanted you to work for him here in the spire, for whatever wages he cared to pay, you would do it willingly or the pig-men would use… persuasion. But in fact, when the red gold began to appear, the pay was good. Not that there was really anywhere to spend it."

"You are all free to go now," Adara told them. "Back to your homes, or to leave Kragstein entirely and seek out someplace where your accumulated wages will allow you to lead a comfortable life. But Hildy, I know that some of the employees here were happily working on the Mancer King's behalf, and abusing their fellow staff members. Before I allow the rest of the staff to leave, I hope you will be able to point them out to me."

"There was one I know of," Gudrun said with a malicious gleam in her eye. "Sigmund, who brought us our meals in the concubines' quarters, would use me sexually several times a week. He wouldn't let me eat until I had serviced him." She looked to her fellow former concubines, who nodded in agreement. They, too, had been abused by the same man.

Hildy's eyes widened, and her kindly, plump features took on a cold look. "I had no idea," she said quietly. "But I never liked that man. He was always eyeing the girls in the kitchen." She gestured around the room. "The living quarters are sexually segregated. Members of the staff who were romantically involved would get together in some of the un-tenanted areas of the spire during daylight hours. But to be caught doing that was death."

She went on, "Two others that I know of were held in higher esteem by the master. Roger Dubois was supposedly like a butler, the chief of the human staff. He reported every misstep to Sarand, and sometimes after he had told on people they would just… disappear. He was the only one of us allowed out into town, and he was the one who'd bring Sarand new girls if he spotted one that he knew the master would enjoy."

The two other former concubines nodded. "He was the one that brought me here," the redhead said. "Papa would have killed him, if he hadn't brought along all those Swinzen guards."

"And the third?" Adara asked, relieved to find there had been so few. She'd envisioned having to put half the staff to the sword.

"Ragnar Eriksen," Hildy said, and there was a general chorus of agreement. "A little rat of a man, Roger's toady. He'd do whatever Roger told him to, and keep an eye on the rest of us when Roger was out of the spire. Pretty much all of the women, and the rest of the men, were only working for Sarand because we had no other choice. But those two were right bastards."

Adara nodded. "I'll need someone to come with me who can identify Roger and Ragnar," she said. "Sigmund I already know. But the rest of you are free to gather whatever belongings you have and leave. We plan to lock up the tower for good before we depart."

They brought the good news, and the chance for freedom, to the rest of the female servants in the fourth floor's second apartment.

These were chambermaids, a seamstress, and a team of laundresses – all of whom embraced Adara before making a beeline for the stairs leading down. They gathered in the hallway on the ground floor, told to wait until Ferdyn came to unlock the outer doors for them.

By now the hour was getting late, and the rescuers found the men in their single apartment on the third floor already in bed. None of them had realized what had transpired, not even Roger. He and his toady Ragnar had private rooms within the large apartment, whereas Sigmund and the other half dozen men who had served the Mancer King all bunked together in a dormitory.

Gudrun had not gone with the rest of the women, including her two fellow ex-concubines, but instead had gotten into some warm clothing and volunteered to accompany Adara and Ferdyn to the men's apartment. They went into the dormitory first, seizing and binding Sigmund before waking the rest of the men.

Sigmund's cries were quickly stifled with a gag, and it appeared he had not disturbed either Roger or Ragnar as they were binding him. The stone walls of the apartment were thick. They left Sigmund tied down on his bed, and the other six men gathered around dressed in nightshirts.

"Put on your clothes, gentlemen," Adara told them quietly. "We're getting out of here tonight. And keep it down – we don't want Roger and Ragnar to hear." With wolfish expressions the six – ranging in age from early twenties to late forties – quickly got into their clothing. Then their rescuers set about explaining what had happened after they'd finished work this evening.

After the explanation, the eldest of them said, "Dubois and Eriksen have it coming. We'd be happy to see they get it, but we have no weapons." Adara and Ferdyn exchanged glances. Then they began rifling their clothes. Between them they came up with six daggers, and handed them around. Then they retreated to the apartment's living room, and sat in bemused silence listening to the screams. Sensibly, the force had split themselves into two teams of three, opening the two private rooms at the same time so as not to give either occupant warning.

As the raid began, Gudrun asked "Do you have another of those daggers, perchance?" Eyeing her with a hint of trepidation, Ferdyn handed her the last one of the four he usually kept secreted about his person. With a grin that showed too many teeth, the blonde girl took the knife and trotted off down the hall in the direction of the dormitory where they'd left Sigmund tied to the bed. There was some mumbling, and then a stifled shriek.

Within a couple of minutes the six men emerged from the private bedrooms. They'd wiped off the knife blades on the bedclothes of their victims, and now happily handed them back to their owners. Time to go. As they trooped out of the apartment, Adara and Ferdyn stopped in at the dormitory room.

Gudrun, bloody knife in hand, stood grinning down at the still-trussed Sigmund. Surprisingly, the man was still alive. But his nightshirt was rucked up around his armpits, and at his crotch was a gaping, bloody wound. Erg. Both Adara and Ferdyn turned their eyes away, calling "Gudrun! Time to go!"

She looked up, breaking her vengeful trance, and nodded. Then she wiped the knife across Sigmund's nightshirt and turned to follow them out the door. "Uh…?" Adara said, gesturing toward the ruined man on the bed.

"Oh, he'll bleed to death soon enough," the girl answered cheerfully.

The last of Sarand's former unwilling employees had walked out of the bloody tower, and Adara and Ferdyn pulled the gates shut behind them and turned the key in the lock. Then they stood looking at each other in disbelief. They had done it! The entire Bloodspire, top to bottom, held no one but them. Them, and a couple of million marks' worth of gold.

They fell into the best hug they could manage, armored as they both were and slung about with edged weapons. Then, they stood just looking at each other again – grinning from ear to ear. "Whoo!" Adara gasped, making an effort to banish the gruesome images of their slaughtered foes from her memory.

"Indeed," Ferdyn replied. "What next?" "I think we'd better go get the cart and horses out of the stable at the inn," she said seriously. "I don't think we want to be loading up in daylight."

Epilogue

Midmorning found many more travelers than usual on the road between Kragstein and Baadzen – most of them on foot and heading south. In among them, though, was a creaking farm wagon pulled by two large, elderly cart horses. The way was all downhill and the cart appeared to be nearly empty – only a wadded-up tarpaulin and a couple of canvas packs in it; yet the horses seemed to be making heavy going of it.

It was driven by a pair of lumpy-looking rustics, bundled up against the cold in a mismatched collection of rough-spun garments. The woman, hunched over as if with great age, had most of her face covered by a dusty scarf. What could be seen of it seemed puckered and scarred as if by some scrofulous affliction.

She leaned her head tiredly against her companion's shoulder, yawning. "When we get back to the Maridem's Waters," Adara murmured, "I'm going to soak in the bath for an hour and then sleep for a week." The driver put an arm around her and gave her an affectionate squeeze.

"Sounds like a good idea," he said with an answering yawn. "Let's sleep for a week, and then stay in bed for another two days." She squeezed him back.

The End
(for now...)

www.ingramcontent.com/pod-product-compliance
Lightning Source LLC
Chambersburg PA
CBHW071246130626
46556CB00003B/1190